D1606097

Loose Ends

Loose Ends

Short Stories Started
During the Vietnam War

James N. Zitzelsberger

(:c)

Moki Lane Publishing
Oshkosh, WI

© *2013 by James N. Zitzelsberger*

Loose Ends
is a collection of fictional short stories. All characters, plots, settings and themes are products of the author's imagination or interpretation. Any semblance to actual events, places or persons, living or dead, is coincidental.

Suggested Cataloging:

Zitzelsberger, James N., 1948-
Loose ends : short stories started during the
Vietnam War / James N. Zitzelsberger. 1st ed.
p. cm.
1. Vietnam War, 1961-1975—Fiction. 2. United States.
Navy—Seabees—Fiction. 3. United States. Navy. Mobil
Construction Battalions—Fiction. 4. United States. Navy—
Military life—Fiction. 5. Short stories—Seabees—Fiction.
I. Title.
DDC 808.83 (Fic) 959.704

Library of Congress Control Number:
2013910325

ISBN: (10) 0-989-41050-1
(13) 978-0-9894105-0-2

First Edition

Moki Lane Publishing
1199 E. Black Wolf Avenue,
Oshkosh, Wisconsin 54902

www.mokilane.com

Printed on acid-free paper by
ECPrinting, Eau Claire, Wisconsin

This book is dedicated to
Kateri Renee *and* **Jack Carlyle**

My sincere appreciation goes to

Mary Klein, Elaine Durman and Aaron Zitzelsberger

for insight and assistance.

Thank you!

Contents

Preface

Pete Seeger once said, "You can't have a light without a dark to put it in." The short stories that follow are like that inasmuch as they are a little lighter than the standard dark fare from the Vietnam War. They are not a record of accomplishments by the Seabees of the United States Navy— that record speaks for itself! Rather, this is a perspective based upon serving in a Seabee battalion. The stories are fictional snapshots from a time and place that changed minds and lives. The changes were not abrupt but more piecemeal like the assignments and forces that ebbed and flowed through orders, actions, reactions and reflections. Coping skills were, of course, essential armaments because it was serious business as only war can be—but also monkey business as only young men can make it.

The main character, Henry James Barthochowski (Cow, for short), is a Wisconsin farm boy—a listener, observer and anything but a cheerleader for military decorum. Young and impressionable, his enlistment unfolds during a time of social unrest and national uncertainty that even permeates the military. Cow knows how to follow orders, but he also knows how to look around, behind and through them as only a kid can. And a kid he is, like so many others with two tours in Vietnam before turning 21 years of age.

Looking back, the truth about why we were in Vietnam is still elusive. Getting in was apparently easier than getting out and many participants still look over their shoulders trying to understand how, why or where they fit in. Some search for patterns in the murky light of their minds while others seek resolution through family, friends and fellowship. If the half-life of a war is one generation, the uncertainty and introspection created during that time will be with us for many years to come.

The Tet Offensive of 1968 is now nearly a half-century behind us and some of our soldiers have been gone that long or longer. Indeed, the children they left behind may already be grandparents. It is a long time to be looking back because details shift, points dull and memories merge in the kaleidoscope of time. Through that lens, actions and perspectives change and coalesce in review of what we did, how it was done, who we were and what we have become.

To the heroes who did not come home, may God bless and keep you. For those lost since, may you rest in peace. For all who have served, thank you!

James N. Zitzelsberger

May 27, 2013

Loose Ends

I

Marvin

MKE was a dead end on his way home. The last flight had left, or never come in, and the final bus had pulled out long before midnight. For a while, Cow wandered around the airport killing time by looking in windows of locked shops at things he could not afford. Later, he sat and dozed on a double bench in the middle of the concourse until finally, curled up in his pea coat, he fell asleep.

"There's no sleeping here, sailor," woke him with a nightstick pushed against his ribs.

Sitting up quickly, Cow looked at the officer through sleepy eyes and said, "Sorry, but there's no place to go." The man in blue gave him an indifferent look, shrugged his shoulders and walked away slapping the stick against his open palm.

The clock above the counter in the coffee shop said 3:55 when Cow dropped his seabag and sat down on a stool. In front of him, an old black man was wiping down the stainless steel coffee maker and Cow could see both of their reflections in the bright finish. The old guy had on a white chef's coat and wore a white paper hat with a thin red stripe near the bottom. The stripe marked where the white hat ended and his white hair began. After a moment, he turned around toward Cow while lifting an order pad from one pocket and a pen from the other.

"What'll it be?" he asked.

"Two eggs and toast."

"And coffee? It'll be done in a minute or two."

"Or water," Cow added smartly, "unless it perks before I'm done and the crowd doesn't drink it all."

"And how would you like those eggs, Sir?" asked the cook with his own smart emphasis on "Sir."

"Over-easy's fine, whatever's easier for you."

"Over-easy it is then," said the cook while scrutinizing the tired face in front of him and adjusting his appraisal from some sarcastic smart-ass to just another kid in uniform.

Turning to the dark steel griddle, he ladled out some corn oil and pushed it back and forth with a spatula. Opening a cooler door, he picked up two eggs in one hand and bumped them hard against the edge of the griddle to crack them open. In the one smooth movement, the eggs dropped into the heated oil and the shells disappeared into a wastebasket below. Reaching in again, he had a third egg in hand before the cooler door had completely closed.

Opening a new loaf of bread, he asked over his shoulder, "Stuck here all night?"

"Yeah," Cow replied to the back in front of him. "I tried to sleep on one of those seats out there for a few minutes, but Mr. Po-Lease Man poked me with his damn stick."

4

"Just his job," said the cook, still facing the griddle. "We get a lot of drunks through here that miss their flights, or miss something, an' it ain't no hotel."

"No, I guess not," said Cow. "But I can't help it if the planes are screwed up. I didn't order the damn snow in Chicago."

Dropping two slices of bread into the toaster, the cook pulled down a screeching, grinding metal lever. "Snow in Chi-town?" he asked while slipping the spatula under each of the eggs to lift their edges and gently turn them over.

"Yeah," said Cow, mentally comparing the three eggs on the griddle against the two he had ordered. "You could see the lights of the planes, stacked one above the other, as far as you could see into the snowy sky. I don't know how they can land and take off like that without an accident."

"They only have one runway open?" asked the cook.

"That's the way it looked."

"Must-a-been lake effect and we didn't get a thing up here. But the lake does that sometimes. Sometimes we get it and they don't. Luck of the draw."

"Yeah," Cow said again, and then added, "almost didn't get here at all. We just missed another plane over New York. Don't know what it was but I saw the bottom of it as it banked past us. It was so close you could see the oil streaks under the engine cowls."

The toast popped up with another squeal but the cook ignored it momentarily while placing the three eggs on a plate.

One piece at a time, he brushed melted butter on the toast before cutting it diagonally and placing it around the eggs. In another slight of hand, he retrieved a sprig of parsley from the cooler and laid it on top before setting the plate in front of Cow.

"I call it the very early morning special. Eat up," he said and turned back to scrape the griddle's hot surface with his spatula. "And the coffee will be done in just a second. Where did you say you were going?"

"Home. Hillton. I've got ten days. And then Gulfport, Mississippi—wherever that is—and Vietnam, I suppose."

"On a ship?" asked the cook, still turned away.

"No, Seabees, in Gulfport. But I don't know how long we'll be there."

The cook filled his cup from the spout of the coffee maker and took a sip. "Just right," he said, and filled another cup nearly to the top. "Black or white?" he asked.

Cow shook his head before he realized he was still looking at the cook's back and muttered, "Black," with his mouth full of toast and eggs.

The coffee cup bumped against his plate as the cook set it down and reached under the counter to pull out a stool. "Had a grandson over there last year. Army. Somewhere around Saigon. I tried to look it up in an atlas once but couldn't find the exact place. He was somewhere in that

Mekong Delta area; but I'm not really sure where. Eleven months with two Purple Hearts and he still couldn't get away."

Cow swallowed and lifted the hot coffee to his lips. Steam rose from the cup in front of his face as he looked through it and listened. It made his eyes water, and, he thought, the cook's too.

"They brought him home last November. My daughter got a little life insurance money but it won't bring Marvin back." He stood up and pushed the stool under the counter as the same officer who had poked Cow with his nightstick came in and took a seat at the end of the counter where he could see everything in the room and out through the door.

"Sleeping Beauty giving you any trouble, Marv?"

"Noooo," said the cook. "He just needs to catch an early plane. What'll you have?"

"Usual," said the officer. "Black."

Cow emptied his own cup and pulled his wallet from his jumper pocket to pay. He was fishing for his last five-dollar bill when the cook motioned with the back of his hand to put his money away.

"On the house," he said, loud enough for the cop to hear. "It's the very early morning special, remember?" The guest check had 'Paid in Full' scribbled across it with the initial 'M' below. "If you've got the first flight, you better get goin' so you don't miss it."

Standing, Cow said, "Thank you," in a sincere voice that probably hit the cook somewhere in the middle of his shoulders because he had already turned back to the coffee pot. Picking up his seabag, Cow glanced at the cop at the end of the counter. He was holding his coffee with both hands while the nightstick rested next to the saucer. Almost through the door, he heard the old man say to the officer, "Marvin's birthday today—he'd-a-been 20...."

II

Jambalaya

Cow lifted his seabag from the turntable nearly as quickly as it dropped from the conveyor. It was the only seabag and his only piece of luggage, if it could be called that. The street-level exit was directly behind him where a line of yellow taxis waited outside beyond the sidewalk. He had hoped to find someone to share the cost of the ride downtown but the airplane had been nearly empty and the other passengers had all but disappeared. He still did not really know where he was going, but, one step at a time, he was getting there: Milwaukee, Chicago, New Orleans, and soon enough, he thought, some place called Gulfport, Mississippi.

It was midafternoon and hot in the bus depot downtown when Cow bought a ticket to Gulfport for less than half of what he paid for the ride from the airport into New Orleans. His money was running low again, as usual, but he would make it and had until midnight to report.

The first seat behind the driver was empty and Cow slid into it. Two women, one black, one white, chatted in the seat behind. The air conditioning in the Greyhound rushed and whistled almost as loudly as on the airplane but he could still hear them talking about babies, families and places he had never heard of: Thibodaux, Plaquemine, Houma. It was almost like being in a foreign land searching for something familiar.

The streets out of New Orleans were narrow and crowded, and the bus turned often before heading east on US 90. But even that highway was a slim two lanes where it left the suburbs and plunged into the mire. East, that much Cow knew by the signs, but any other sense of direction had left him and when the bus leaned into curves, gravity pulled his body with it as though tugging him into the nearly solid swamp on either side. He had never seen anything like it.

From inside the bus, the edge of the road appeared to be lined by a tall marshy-tan wall of grass. Every few miles, it seemed, the bus stopped at what looked to be plank paths cut into the grass, reeds and cattails. Sometimes, someone was waiting to get on; at other times, the driver got out to pick up a package lying along the road or open the belly of the bus to drop something off. At home, in Wisconsin, big swamps might be a couple square miles but they were usually measured in acres. This had to be measured in townships as the quarter-hours slipped by and the morass kept pace.

Long narrow trestle bridges lifted the bus wherever the swamp squeezed out its water. The bridges were old and black with high tops crisscrossed by steel girders that boxed in the whine of the tires. On the approaches, when they came up out of the swamp, Cow could see furthest and was most claustrophobic. There was nothing on the horizon: not a smokestack, water tower, or anything to mark a change in geography and the beginnings of civilization. When the highway dropped back down, he felt like the whole bus was going under.

On what may have been the only straight stretch, the driver slowed the bus and took most of the middle of the road between two lines of semis parked on either side. When the line on the left parted for a moment, Cow could see an unpainted shack, a hundred yards back, with a well-trodden boardwalk cutting through the grass. Red curtains showed plainly in both front windows as the distance between his curiosity and naiveté began to shorten. In the seat behind him, the subject turned to church, disgrace and prayers for the fallen.

Beyond the last tall, black riveted bridge, as if they had come out of a tunnel, a small town opened on the left and a beach on the right began to parallel the highway. The beach was of sun-bleached white sand sloping down to serene, light blue water that laid calm and flat all the way to the horizon. Where the world fell away, the sea blended with the hazy skyline. Intermittently, long weathered piers jutted out into the water with benches and gazeboes on the ends of many.

Cow was fixated on the landlessness of it all until the driver used his PA to point out the huge scenic houses on the other side of the highway. "Summer plantation homes," he said, "many dating back to before the Civil War." The women behind him were quiet now, apparently listening, but Cow soon turned back to the sea and the dark weathered pilings of old piers poking from the sand and water in unspoken ellipses. On nearly every broken or rotted post sat a white seagull. Several miles out, as though on posts of their own, a dozen large white boats with long booms and dark nets, appeared becalmed on the water. Behind him, the two women began talking about shrimp, crabs and jambalaya.

Cow's hands were tight on the metal rail in front of him when the bus made a hard left followed by a quick right swing into a roofed stall that ended against a solid brown brick wall. "Gulfport," the driver announced. Opening the door, he left the microphone dangling from the steering wheel as he stepped out and Cow got up to follow.

The seabag was the first thing pulled from the luggage compartment and dropped on the pavement as Cow came off the bus. When he bent to pick it up, the two women went around him and through a single wood door in the brick wall. Straightening, there was little to see except for the bricks and a night-light burning above the door in the late afternoon. Next to the partially open door was a small sign in the shape of a hand and pointing finger. "Tickets," was painted across the palm of the hand with fancy curlicues and a flourish of white accent over dark shadow.

Cow followed the two women inside where a large, semi-circular counter filled much of the back half of the room. In the front half, a chessboard of black and white tile covered the floor. A row of chairs, like pawns, lined a wide bowed window parallel to the street outside and refolded newspapers lay on the window ledge waiting to be read again.

On the far wall, there were two fountains, one with the water running. On either side of the fountains, two sets of doors identified restrooms with alternating "Men" and "Women" painted on them. The running water was cold and tasteless, as it should be, and Cow straightened while wiping his mouth with the back of his hand. "Biloxi, Ocean Springs, Gautier, Pascagoula and points east now boarding!" called out the ticket agent as he pushed a cart of baggage toward the side door.

The black women came out of the women's door on the left and stepped to the nearest bubbler for a sip of water— the bubbler that was not running and sure to be warm. Cow was about to say something when the white women came out of the women's door on the right and stepped up to the running water. Puzzled for a moment, he lifted eyes in bewilderment until the word "Colored" jumped out at him from above the doors on the left. Painted in large blue-black block letters, the word formed a wide arrow that curved downward to the un-running water between the two doors.

The black woman waited until the white woman finished her drink and they walked out together. Again, still unsure of where to go, Cow followed at a distance past the line of chairs and through the front door. Outside, a black man was leaning against his yellow taxi and Cow asked how far it was to the Seabee base.

"Too far to drag that bag," said the cabby. "I'll take you out there for two bucks. It'll only take a minute or two, but it's too far to walk. Throw your bag in the back. Looks like you're the only one this afternoon."

Pulling away from the curb, they passed the two women walking down the sidewalk. They were still talking but Cow was not sure if he would like jambalaya.

III

McDoogle

Swooping was his invention and consisted of looping around the Doogle Farm to get the lay of the land, parking in the yellow striped back row and mingling with the locals to pick up girls. The Doogle Farm was a facetious sobriquet for an off-base hamburger joint and loose approximation of his own name and needs.

McDoogle's swooping car was a 1960 Chevy two-door with what he called, "A slammin' six-banger and a slush box." In the summer of 1967, it cost three hundred bucks just the way it sat next to a local garage. It was not much to look at in the beginning, but two dozen cans of flat black spray paint and a roll of masking tape began its renovation.

Working in front of the Gulfport barracks, the all-white sedan first became dapple-gray from the window line down. In a couple hours, the narrow, wavy spray began to fill in until the bottom half of the car became a dark, flat, gray-black beneath a white top and pillars. Later the next afternoon, an emery cloth removed any flies and bugs that had dared to settle and a few last puffs of paint erased their pesky trails.

McDoogle found a set of used chrome reverse rims for fifty bucks in the *Gulfport Sun Herald*, and, after regular hours, made the change in the base tire shop. In the process, he turned the old whitewalls to the inside so they would not clash with the shiny rims and put the balancing weights there too. Attention to detail kept everything clean and mean.

The car was beginning to take shape when McDoogle found the local auto parts store carried the same cast iron spring nuts found in his frayed Chicago catalog. The nuts were a poor man's remedy for worn and tired coil springs, but McDoogle saw both their utilitarian and artistic value. He bought four bags of a dozen each and used the bumper jack to gingerly raise each corner of the car until the coiled springs beneath were stretched wide enough to insert the metal cubes. As he let each corner back down, the whole body began to inch up and finally settled nearly half a foot higher than it had been. To the casual observer, the car began to look like it had a custom suspension.

An unintended consequence of having so many metal blocks between the spring coils was that the ride stiffened and rode right up McDoogle's spine unless, of course, he was in the swooping position. In the swooping position, the front seat was pushed all the way back and the driver cantilevered most of his butt out over the front edge of the seat until his back formed an arc between the cushion and the backrest with his eyeballs barely peering above the dash. Since McDoogle was over six feet tall, to get so low in the seat he had to cross his legs and used his left foot on the accelerator and the right one on the brake. From the outside looking in, only his hat appeared to be sitting on the window ledge. From the inside looking out, the spokes of the steering wheel framed his field of vision.

McDoogle was a Renaissance man in many respects. As a mechanic, artist and musician, he found the sound of his creation lacking and gave it a tune-up with a hammer and awl. Parking one side on the curb, he crawled into the gutter beneath the car and punched twenty holes into the front quarter of the muffler. When he started the engine, the sound was impressive and the motor took on the loud, guttural roar of a racing engine twice its size. For perfect pitch, he punched another half dozen holes near the center to bring out the music of the master.

With all those notes under the hood, it was obvious to McDoogle, although not to everyone around him, that an adjustment was needed to let the sound resound. Being an alternative thinker, while his buddies were gawking and skylarking, McDoogle was absorbed with the hood hinges and corresponding math. Multiplying the length of the three bolts on each side by forty washers each, he dropped the hood and went roaring off to the hardware store. In twenty minutes, he was back with everything he needed for three dollars and ninety-six cents. USAC would have been proud of him. In one quick pit stop, the old bolts were pulled and replaced with the new longer ones to hold the washers between the hinge and the hood. The net result was that the back edge of the hood became a full three inches higher than the fenders and cowling with plenty of room for air to get in, the music to get out and curiosity to peak.

McDoogle had been swooping in and out of the Doogle Farm almost every night looking for a burger, fries and thighs. At first, the old Chevy did not get much attention, but after he put on the rims, raised her a little and heightened the hood, some heads started turning.

Two chrome tailpipe extensions were soon added beneath the rear bumper, one for exhaust and the other for symmetry. As a result, because the approach to the Doogle Farm sloped down sharply from the sidewalk to the street, McDoogle had to be careful going in and out to avoid a howling, screeching serenade that might rip off both the extensions and the tailpipe. This became especially critical if he had a couple girls in the back seat. He found, however, that a little extra push on the throttle, spin of the steering wheel and touch of the brake pedal would lift and bank the turning car outward to keep its underside away from the concrete. It also took enough weight off the inside tire to make it spin and squeal louder than the giggling girls behind him.

In little more than a month, the Chevy became a swooping sensation. The chrome reverse wheels and black-wall tires with brake fluid glaze looked wet, slippery and intimidating while the wedge of the raised hood intrigued the uninitiated. For those who tried to peek into the darkness beneath the hood to see what was in there, McDoogle's self-deprecating mantra was always the same: "She ain't no go-fast." The car was a conversation piece, a starting point, a beginning from which McDoogle could say, "Hey, ya-wanna go for a ride?" And if the girl or girls said yes, everyone jumped in with a laugh, slunk down in the seats and went roaring off into the Mississippi night with one squealing tire and sometimes a shower of sparks from the still scraping extensions.

It was all working well and catching on with a few others until McDoogle asked Jerome to jump in for a swoop-of-the-loop. McDoogle probably never gave it a second thought and Jerome may not have either because he came from the northwest, a long way from Mississippi in the sixties. In that turn of events, though, the first excited waves from the locals shrank to limp limbs and glaring stares. Three cars were already pulling out by the time McDoogle came around for the second time. Looking for a parking spot, he followed the departing taillights for a moment before backing into the middle of the vacated spaces. Turning off the engine, with the windows down, he was surprised at how quiet it had become as he and Jerome climbed out of the Chevy, each giving his door a gentle shove to close.

Inside, the air-conditioning felt cold and the young white woman behind the counter only asked McDoogle what he wanted. "Burger, fries and a Coke," he said, as always, without picking up on the frosty reception. The single order was tapped into the cash register and the girl turned to the machines behind her. While she worked, a man and woman came in and stood behind Jerome. He was next, but when McDoogle's order was handed to him, she skipped Jerome and spoke around him to the people next in line.

McDoogle stood there realizing, for the first time, what was happening and began to read the anger on Jerome's face. He was about to say, "Here, take these..." when a crash of glass from outside caught his ear and he found himself looking past Jerome's turning head toward an echoing thump, thump, thump beyond the glass windows. "What the hell?" he said, as Jerome put his dark hand on McDoogle's shoulder and pulled him toward the door.

Outside, five young men with baseball bats were sitting on the hoods of their cars and the open space on either side of the swooping car was littered with glass sparkling in the yellow light. Even from a hundred feet away, McDoogle could see that the headlights, windshield and the back window were all gone. Getting closer, he could also see that the ball bats had dark gray paint on their ends from where they hit the hood, doors, and trunk.

In the deathly silence, the Coke in McDoogle's hand slipped and fell on the blacktop with an ironic explosion of sweet spray that coated the glittering glass. Jerome opened one dented door, brushed glass from the seat and got in. McDoogle dug into his pocket for the keys and followed on the driver's side. They sat upright now and slowly pulled out of the Doogle Farm without so much as a scrape, squeal or giggle from behind. With no windshield, the almost cool night air of Mississippi hit both of them square in the face.

IV

Novotny

The Starlifter rotated slowly on the tarmac half a world away from Gulfport. The airplane had flown through twelve time zones in one long night to bring two hundred Seabees to Da Nang and take Novotny back.

The men slouched in web seats along both outer walls with plywood sheeting for backrests. It had been a hard ride with pallets of gear forming a mountain range between them and what little space remained was for feet, legs and stumbling when someone needed to take a trip to the head. For light, three bare bulbs cast long yellow shadows that jaundiced the men and the mountains.

Cow had brought along a paperback to pass the time but there was not enough light to read. At first, there had been a lot of nervous chatter, but, as time wore on, the noise wore down and the quiet of thought took over. Novotny's flight over must have been nearly the same and Cow, in turn, found himself thinking about the two little girls waiting at home for their daddy. In his musing, he could see them jumping around on the back seat of their father's canary-yellow Barracuda. Novotny was always telling them to sit down and keep their feet off the seats but it seldom worked. Once, when Cow had been standing behind him and winked at the girls being told to

23

sit down, they began to make faces at their daddy until everyone nearby was roaring with laughter, even Novotny.

But no one was laughing now. Novotny had been on the Advanced Team, three weeks ahead, and it seemed like a lifetime since they left. Cow had heard the rumors about life expectancy in Vietnam, but it was mostly speculation and there was no way to know if any of it was true. The only truth now was that he and the rest of his company were finally there and Novotny was already going home. From where Cow sat in the twilight of the turning transport, nothing was clearer than that.

In the third grade, a classmate had been absent for a week when the teacher finally said that the girl had run across a farm field, became entangled in a barbed wire fence and tore her face, arms, and legs. For nights after that disclosure, a bloodied face appeared in Cow's dreams with hands ripped and legs scraped raw. In his sling seat with eyes closed, Novotny rode with him—bloodied, red and raw.

The first touchdown of their night flight had been so soft that Cow did not realize they were on the ground until the reversers rumbled and the rapid deceleration pulled him forward. Moments later, the plane began turning at short intervals and the blind swings made Cow's stomach move with them. When the plane parked, the pilot announced that it was 10:45 at night, Alaskan time, and thirty-eight degrees in Anchorage. Refueling would take an hour with bathrooms and box lunches waiting inside the hanger. Also, since a new crew was coming on board, he wished the best of luck to everyone. Cow wondered if Novotny had gotten the same message.

Nearly everyone on the airplane was hungry and a little queasy from the hard right angle turns after landing. Their last meal had been in the late afternoon and few had eaten as they finished last-minute affairs and farewells. They had mustered at 5:00 and boarded buses for the three-mile ride to Keesler AFB. It was a short trip, fifteen minutes at most, leaving nearly two hours to kill. At first, they stood around before settling down on their duffel bags to wait. Later, they walked around on the tarmac talking about home and ahead.

Muster and roll call were formalities until what turned out to be the final formation before boarding. Up to then, Cow would have said that Vietnam was still one whole day away; but that notion exploded as "We regret to inform you…" began to echo up and down the rows of men. The regret was that Kevin K. Novotny, EO2, had been killed in the service of his country. Faces remained tight and bodies taut in the silence that followed until, almost riding upon it, the whine of jet engines turned attention away from the platoon leaders to the Starlifter already on the ground and taxiing toward them.

The Anchorage lunch was a ham sandwich, an apple, a bag of chips and a cookie: not much for eight hours. Like many others, Cow took two cans of pop and put one in his jacket pocket to fill the void a little later. Soon, however, another formation broke the respite and, after roll call, the men were marched out to the waiting airplane. As if on cue, or déjà vu, a light colored Plymouth Barracuda sat under a yellowish outside light near the exit door. The car kept heads turning and slowed down the line in the cold night air until someone finally shouted, "Keep moving! Hurry up, it's not yellow."

Cow had been thinking about keeping his Timex set to Central Standard Time while he was in Vietnam so he could know approximately what was happening back home. The watch was hard to read in the low light of the airplane, but their first lift-off had been at 7:58 p.m. as near as he could tell, and they were about to leave Anchorage at a little before 4:00 in the morning, Central Standard Timex Time (CSTT). He could not remember if Novotny wore a watch, but when he held the Timex to his ear, he could hear the seconds beating with the fleeting rapidity of a heart.

Between Anchorage and Tokyo, the cockpit doors were opened and the men in transit invited to crawl up the front ladder to see the operation of the airplane firsthand. A few at a time went forward and came back humbled by the number of gauges and the vast darkness beyond the windshield. The navigator, with his own table, sat behind the co-pilot drawing intersecting lines on a map. Where the lines had taken them closest to Russia, he said an enemy escort had flown alongside.

At 11:35 a.m., CSTT, the C-141 landed in Japan, somewhere outside Tokyo. It was 2:35 in the morning, JST, and there were no cars parked outside the hanger this time, not even a military jeep in the dark of night. Inside, however, the lights were harshly bright illuminating another line of bathroom doors and a couple long tables piled high with the same white cardboard lunch boxes. Cow tried to take two more cans of soda from the cooler but an orderly stopped him this time. "Sorry," he was told, "only one, those are my orders, ya know how it is." Cow knew how it was, and it was only another twenty-four hundred miles to pick up Novotny.

Estimated arrival in Da Nang, South Vietnam, was 5:30 p.m., CSTT. Five hours after takeoff from Tokyo, the Starlifter finished its taxi, made a final turn and came to a stop. Cow had been right on target and it had been twenty-two hours since they boarded the aircraft in Gulfport, Mississippi the evening before. A half hour later, the rear cargo ramp was lowered and the exit doors opened. Almost instantly, the air changed with the heat and humidity of Southeast Asia hitting them as they stepped into the bright morning sunlight. Below, well to the side of the stair, an airman was hunched over the steering wheel of his tow motor waiting for the men to disembark and get their gear out of the way. Hooked to the tow and trailing behind, Cow counted six carts, each loaded with four man-sized boxes, and his wrist was rigid under the band of his Timex as he came down the stair holding a salute to Novotny and the others.

V

Sniper

The Master Chief mainly holed up in his office during the rainy season. In pressed greens and polished black boots, he remained an anomaly, a throwback to homeport where inspections required sharp creases, spit-shines, polished brass and whitewalls around the ears. His office, upstairs at the south end of the service shop, was as far away as it could be from the grease rack, dirty tires and muddy floor to the north where a virtual DMZ of mechanical misfits and operator's complaints vied for attention.

This was not on the front lines of Vietnam, but a sandbar southeast of Da Nang that held off the South China Sea on one side and overlooked the Vu Gia River with its brown muddy wash on the other. When the weather was dry, the sandbar was a sandbar and the sand ruled; but during the rainy season, the silty sand turned to mud and the mud held sway. Sandbags, corrugated metal, wood planks and scraps of cardboard made makeshift walkways until even they were swamped by the enveloping mud.

The mud clung to boots, pants, hands and faces as the color of equipment in the shop changed from olive drab to cocoa-brown. When wet vehicles came in, the mud dripped and puddled before hitchhiking across the floor on boots and cuffs. Hands were smeared with it and coffee cup handles

29

became coated, layered, hardened and formed to the muddy fingers that held them.

Up in his office, the Master Chief was above the morass and only occasionally, perhaps when the walls began to close in on him, did he come down with his clean coffee cup in one hand and a notebook in the other. His intention, it seemed, was always the same: to probe the morale of his troops. Morale, however, was not nearly as high as his office and it usually did not take long before some unsuspecting Seabee was up to his ears in ire for not meeting the Master Chief's standards of dedication to duty.

The term "Seabee" is something of a fleshed out initialism taken from the first letters of Construction Battalion (CB) and depicted by a rotund bumblebee wearing a sailor's hat while holding construction tools and a machine gun. The Seabee slogan is "We Build, We Fight" and the units are kin to the Marines and Army Engineers. When the Master Chief came down in his clean greens and starched hat, he looked a lot like an inflated bumblebee carrying the tools of his trade, sans the machine gun.

Benny Beecher was thumbing through his stash of comic books when he happened to turn his head and caught sight of the Master Chief descending the stairs. Benny's brand of coping with being in Vietnam was what he called "studying for chief"—a rank for which he had absolutely no desire—and his study materials consisted of a stack of comic books that he kept in the cabs of the vehicles he was supposed to be greasing. Watching the Master Chief come down the stairs, he pushed his entertainment under the seat, opened the door and slid out of the cab focused and engaged.

The muddy truck sat on top of two wide concrete walls, four feet high, with an alley between for changing oil, greasing u-joints and general maintenance from below. A line for the air-operated grease gun snaked down the alley beneath the truck and lay idle on the floor, full of air, waiting for Benny to complete his study above and get back to work. But work was never Benny's priority, and, as soon as his feet hit the floor, he was moving for mischief.

On the sandbar of East Da Nang, snipers were a rare sight and seldom stopped in unless they were looking for something. Unfettered, they roamed the country at will with scoped high-powered rifles and camouflaged fatigues. They were tough, wily, accurate and usually in need of a shower. Benny fit the profile and personality even if he did not have a high-powered rifle. What he did have, however, was an air-operated grease gun, motivation and oncoming target.

By the time the Master Chief stepped on the floor and began his roam through the shop, Benny had already sidled up to the grease gun cabinet at the end of the alley and twisted the air valve clockwise for maximum pressure. Slipping back beneath the truck, he took cover behind a front wheel and found a tie-rod grease zerk above his head. With a quick coupling and finger pull, he gave the zerk a shot of grease at full air, which caused the rubber cover on the top side to erupt with a spray of mud, dirt and grease onto his cap, face and shoulders. Rubbing his quickly watering eyes to clear them, he swiped his dirty wetted fingers across his cheeks and the muddy war paint added camouflage.

Surveying his kingdom, the Master Chief came forward nearing Benny's field of fire but was still 5 yards out of range. With another glance up at the tie-rod end and his finger on the trigger, Benny watched the distance close. At maximum air, he could grease a target at twenty-five yards and the tool crib door, where the Master Chief was apparently heading, was only twenty. With rifle range expertise, Benny set the handle of the grease gun on the concrete wall, took a deep breath and waited. One shot was all he was going to get and then he had to blend in with his surroundings.

Facing outward, in the middle of the tool crib door, was Eddie Olson. Eddie, somewhat like Benny, was also absorbed in a book but did not see the Master Chief coming toward him. He liked to read and preferred the paperback biographies and histories he sometimes found at the China Beech USO. Unlike Benny, however, Eddie already had one warning from the Master Chief concerning "idleness and responsibility in the face of the communistic threat and America's war effort in Southeast Asia." It was something he had not forgotten although the books held his attention too.

When Eddie looked up, he froze as the Master Chief stopped in front of him. His book rested on the shelf of the tool crib's Dutch door and, with his left eye, he could see the red flush of anger already rising from the Chief's neck to his forehead. With his other eye, his right, he could see past the Master Chief and instantly recognized the barrel of the grease gun resting on the concrete wall below the curvature of the truck's front tire. The barrel, foreshortened, flared into the shape of a hand and melted into a cocoa colored collage where the truck fender overshadowed a tire and dirty smeared face. The blending was almost perfect.

With a muzzle velocity of a hundred feet per second, breath out, Benny squinted down the barrel with his right eye, left eye tight shut. Aiming for the middle of the Master Chief's collar, he pulled the trigger. Unfortunately, though, because his left eye was closed, he did not see Charlie Weeks striding up on that side.

As much an artist and athlete as an assassin, the moment the grease gun spit with its pronounced double puff of air, Benny let out a loud, "Damn!" while performing a pirouette that ended with the tip of the grease gun tight up against the previously scouted tie-rod end. From twenty yards and a split second away, his assumed position was one of "nose-to-the-grindstone" and attention to detail.

They say you never hear the bullet that hits you and some say you never feel it either—at least not at first. It took the gob of grease a good half second to cover the twenty-plus yards with plenty enough time for Charlie Weeks to step behind the Master Chief squarely into Benny's field of fire. Unlike the pontifications, however, Charlie did feel the thump in the middle of his back and promptly turned around to see who wanted him. The Master Chief, hearing Benny's outburst of "Damn!" also sensed something behind him and jerked around to look too. His sudden turn broke the pencil he was using to write Eddie's name in his notebook and it left a gray-black smear down the page to where the paper was torn from the lead digging in.

The newly formed line now had Eddie in back, Charlie Weeks in front and the Master Chief sandwiched between with his nose almost touching the grease soaking into the back of Charlie's shirt. Being considerably shorter than Charlie, the Master Chief peered first at the grease and then rose on his tiptoes to look over Charlie's shoulder toward the grease rack. In the alley, under the truck, Benny was wiping more dirt off his smeared face with his free hand while continuing to point the grease gun toward the conspiratorial tie-rod end with the other.

Behind the Master Chief, Eddie quickly slid his book out of sight and sat waiting with folded hands on the shelf of the Dutch door. Tapping Charlie on the shoulder, the Master Chief pointed out the grim evidence of working on equipment and reminded him to be sure to have a clean shirt on at muster the next morning. Turning back to Eddie, he found only a mutilated page in his notebook, a nearly empty and cold coffee cup and the other half of his broken pencil. Eddie's book was gone and the steam rose even higher in the already red pudgy face. "Get busy," the Chief growled, "clean this place up and don't let me see you sitting here again with nothing to do."

Returning to his office, the Master Chief gave wide berth to the grease rack where Benny was diligently rocking the muddy tie-rod above his head. In his peripheral vision, he watched the Chief pass while continuing to mimic a search for signs of wear and tear. Later, he would buy Charlie Weeks a couple beers to cover the muffed shot and stained shirt.

VI

Puff

Shiell leaned against the sandbags of his open bunker peering into the night sky. The bunker was on top of the sandbank overlooking the river but the action had been going on since midnight much farther out. Nobody knew exactly what was happening but air support had arrived, flares popped and tracers flew. In the distance, the hum of a small spotter plane rose and fell as it circled to drop its flare canisters. Below, in the field of their light, errant tracers sometimes lifted above the brush and tall grass like exclamation points in the prone position.

Several octaves below the spotter but considerably higher in the sky, the low slow drone of a much bigger airplane had entered the darkness and Shiell's ears. There were no lights on either of the aircraft, nothing to attract fire, nothing to see, only noises in the moonless night: phantoms, hovering and covering, there and nowhere. As the heavier drone came on the higher hum departed and the parachuted flares burned themselves out on the way down. As the last one winked out, the night turned back to black.

Richard Jordan Gatling patented his rapid firing gun in 1862. It had six barrels and the "Gatling Gun" was capable of firing one hundred rounds per minute. At the time, like many inventions of war, the carnage it inflicted was considered so horrible it would end wars. A hundred years later, three of Gatling's offspring mounted in an old AC-47 gave new meaning to infliction. Each of the new guns could fire 100 rounds per second and, combined, put out eighteen thousand rounds per minute.

The airplane with its electronically operated armaments was originally nicknamed Spooky, but quickly assumed the somewhat magical sobriquet of Puff, as in *Puff the Magic Dragon*. It was a fitting analogy of time and place: innocent on the outside but the mother of all dragons on the inside. With the guns blazing and buzzing like a rattlesnake's tail, the tongue of the fire-breathing monster stretched all the way to the ground in what looked like one solid red line. Rumor had it that Puff could put a bullet into every square foot of a football field in a minute and a half. Arithmetic adds ten seconds.

Tracers, hollow backed bullets filled with magnesium and strontium, ignite from the friction of passing through the barrel of a gun and burn red from exposure to oxygen in the air. The three guns spit out sixty tracer rounds per second and the pilot, wearing night vision goggles, could follow the red lines all the way to the target on the ground. The real gun sights were only pieces of tape on the pilot's left window that he aligned with the wingtip and target below. By banking the airplane and circling overhead, he remained on target and could fill the area with lead.

The intense red line of tracers was mesmerizing from a distance and reminded Shiell of the red ink that always seemed to streak down the pages of his high school compositions. Not far removed from that time, he could also see the red chalk lines on the chemistry blackboard, bright and steady like mercury in a thermometer, until someone erased them, top to bottom. When Puff's guns stopped, the red line of tracers disappeared as though wiped from the blackboard of night, top down.

Gatling may have been appalled at the ferocity of his creation during the Civil War, but Shiell took it all in stride. "Puff's just another advance on the march toward democracy," he said in his deadpan way the next morning. "After all, the Gatling gun is nothing new," and he told about a collector in his hometown who had an original. "Each summer, he dresses in a Civil War uniform and brings the gun to the 4th of July parade. Every so often, he cranks off ten or twelve blank rounds as the high-wheeled piece rides down Main Street on a hay wagon. The sound from the sidewalk is deafening as the bark of the bullets makes one big, loud, nerve-wracking stutter. Can you imagine?"

Thinking back to the night before, Shiell said he could picture the barrels revolving and imagine the cranks being turned on the guns inside the airplane. It was Independence Day all over with the five-minute flares floating down, the drone from above and the buzz of the barrels.

Later in the afternoon, over beers in the EM Club, Puff's red lines in the night sky began to infiltrate the eyes of the Seabees who had spent the night in their bunkers and worked the whole next day. Shiell, on his third or fourth can of Ballantine, was moving forward in his thinking and said to anyone listening, "Wouldn't it be neat if we could play Puff with our M-16's? I wonder what would happen if we shot nothing but tracers? I'll bet it'd be one hell of a show, wha-da-ya think?"

"I think you're crazy," said Marris from two chairs away. "But that ain't nothin' new," and he chuckled aloud over his chiding remark. Marris rode with Shiell sometimes but never changed his opinion about him. "Besides, where are you going to get all those tracers?"

"I'm just going to raid the ammo box and then take it back and say, 'Hey, look at this, this box ain't got no tracer rounds in it, can you give me a new one? How-da-ya think that happened anyway?' And you know what, the Gunny's gonna do? The Gunny's gonna just give me a new box of ammo and I'll be on my way."

"You should have been there to see it!" Marris said, two days later.

"See what?" someone asked, "What're you talkin' about?"

"The tracers," Marris said. "Shiell brought along five clips with nothin' but tracers and blasted 'em off in the quarry.

You should have seen it—he had 'er on full automatic and it looked like a pile of lava burning in the gravel. Said he could keep 'er lit-up and he did too. The barrel got so hot it started to turn red and it took off all the bluing. You should have seen it!"

Shiell came in and strolled to the bar past the table where Marris sat. He was whistling *Puff the Magic Dragon* as he passed and Marris broke into such a fit of laughter that his eyes watered as he ran out of breath and doubled over.

"You..., you..., you should have seen it," he croaked between gasps for air. "A hundred red tracers and the barrel so hot it melted the bluing. The inside looks like the barrel from hell—pitch black and not a groove left in it—melted that sucker right down. Talk about a fire fight!"

Shiell came back just as Marris stopped long enough to take a sip of his beer. As he got closer, Shiell picked up the tune again and Marris instantly choked with beer dribbling out both sides of his mouth.

"A little late," Shiell said, pulling up a chair, "can't see it anymore. Had to take my rifle over to the armory for a quick look-see. Gunny said he never saw anything quite like it. 'Me either,' I said. 'Took it out to give it a damn cleanin' 'cause it rides around in the truck gettin' dirty, but I sure didn't expect it to look like this. The Gunny said it wasn't safe anymore and they couldn't have me goin' out with a weapon that wasn't safe, so he gave me a new one. I told him I was most certainly appreciative but all he said was to take care of the new one or he'd have to look a little deeper down that barrel. Now wha-da-ya think he meant by that?"

VII

Convoy

The windshield, covered and crated, lay down across the hood to protect it from breaking or glaring in the sun. Tire pressure had been checked for the umpteenth time and the heavy hood was up for one more final inspection. The dump truck had been sitting alongside Highway 1 since 6:00 a.m. and, four hours later with the sun searing the dark painted metal, it still sat there.

Willy counted twenty vehicles in front and twenty behind, but that was only as far as he could see. What he knew was that they were getting nowhere fast. "God, I'm getting hungry," he said. "We should have brought something along but I thought we'd be in Phu Bi by noon, not sitting here wishing we were in Phu Bi. How long can it take that sweeper to make the trip?"

Cow did not answer because there was no way to know. They would start when the sweeper stopped. "Better safe than sorry," he finally said, closing the hot metal hood and blowing on his fingers. Cow was the mechanic—Willy was the driver.

Both sat down in the sand on the shady side of the truck and leaned back against the front tire. Cow asked, "Did you see that jackass at the club last night?"

"Yeah," said Willy, "kind of makes you want to stop drinking. But I didn't stay 'til closing. Was he cryin' in his beer again?"

"Yeah, but I'm beginning to think he's got a few screws loose. I couldn't listen to all that bullshit about how she's pining away without him. Can you guess how many guys have been given the 'heave-ho' since we've been over here? Don't see any of them moping around every time they pop-a-top."

"*Pop a top, again....*" sang Willy. "I like that song and maybe we should have packed an ammo box with PBR's."

"The ultimate weapon," said Cow. "Pabst Blue Ribbon to the rescue! I can just see it on the front page of *The Stars and Stripes:* 'Two Seabees Canned on Convoy!' But if we don't get goin' pretty soon, that bottle may not make it over the mountains."

Highway 1 had no center stripe, not even in the paved places. Mostly sand and dirt, it twisted its dusty way through the mountains north of Da Nang where flat concrete pillboxes, built by the French to guard the bridges, dotted the road. But that was old history and there were no guards at the bridges now. Where machine gun barrels should have been sticking out of the portals there were only dark vacant openings in the concrete. The bridges were not nearly as commanding or sturdy either. Blown up and rebuilt almost weekly, they shook as the trucks crept over toward safer ground.

While Willy drove, Cow surveyed the countryside from the right seat. Without the windshield, the canvas top was gone too leaving only the headache pan from the dump box to keep the sun off them. As they gained altitude, Cow began counting the military vehicles strewn along the mountainside below. "Twenty-nine," he said at one point. "And those are only the ones that haven't been grown over."

Once, when he leaned out over the edge of the door, he could see the last bridge they had crossed behind them. Trucks were still working their way over it and, surprisingly, it still held. Beyond the bridge, all the way to where the road curved back around the mountain, more trucks and clouds of dust came forward. The dust rose behind each truck, but then, as if it got tired of following, began to settle down until the next truck pushed it over the edge of the mountain and raised a new cloud of its own.

Willy drove through the dust carefully and stayed close to the truck ahead because he could no longer see the edge of the road. They were still climbing and the temperature was going down as they went up. Army infantry marched along on the inside, the high side of the road, humping their packs, weapons and ammunition.

"How'd you like to be one of those poor bastards?" asked Cow.

"That's why I joined the Navy," said Willy. "To get on a ship and stay out of Vietnam."

Thick clouds covered the north side of the mountain and they drove into them as they neared the top. Cow liked the cool damp fog, but Willy kept pulling off his glasses to wipe them on his shirt. "I wonder if the idiot who took down this windshield ever thought about driving in the fog, wind and rain?" Letting up on the throttle, he touched the brake lightly and they came to another stop. "Probably can't see the landing strip in front of us," he said. "Give me a swig."

Cow reached under the seat and pulled out the bottle of brandy. He held it up by the neck to peer through it before unscrewing the cap and passing it over. Willy took a small sip through nearly closed lips and handed it back. He wiped his mouth with the side of his hand and the side of his hand on the leg of his pants. "Damn, that's good!" he said.

Cow took a sip too before putting the bottle back under the seat. His Timex said it was 3:00 p.m. "How many miles," he asked?

Willy looked at the odometer. "Thirty-one. Another ten or fifteen, I guess. And here we go." The infantry had kept marching when the trucks stopped, and a couple men were near the front fender when they started forward again.

Cow asked, "What'd you suppose they'd give for a little of our brandy?" Willy did not answer this time because the highway was narrow and he had to keep the truck between the men and mountain on the left and the edge of the road on the right.

"Ya know," he said a few minutes later, "I think we just started going downhill because we've picked up a little speed. We're almost up to ten now!"

A tall dead tree slid past on the right, a gray eerie ghost in the cloudy white. Cow thought he could almost reach out and touch it, but did not. Instead, he thought of booby traps and land mines like the one that got Novotny; and that made him reach under the seat for the bottle just as they came out of the clouds into bright sunlight. They were indeed going downhill and a lush green savanna spread out below them. On the right, a thousand feet below, the dark blue water of the South China Sea filled a cove and washed onto a white sand beach. "God, this is a beautiful place," he said. "Too bad it's so fucked up."

"Stick your toe in that water and one of those sea snakes will grab it and you too," said Willy. "Then we'll see how pretty you think it is."

"I hear they've got your buddy diving for specimens."

"Yeah, I heard that too. How many?"

"How many what?"

"How many trucks or whatever you've been counting over the edge?"

Cow chuckled. "I guess I forgot about them when we got high in the sky. Ya can't count 'em if ya can't see 'em. Or maybe that Aye-Rist-Toe-Krat Brandy covered 'em up." He reached out and turned the outside mirror inward to look at himself. A dirty dark brown face stared back. "Jesus," he said, "I guess sweat and dust does make mud." Lifting his helmet, his forehead was pale where it had been covered. "What'd ya think if I did some finger painting?" Wetting two fingers in his mouth, he made two smears on each cheek. "Wahoo," he said, and then, "Tick-tack-toe," when he crisscrossed the first lines.

Willy looked over and shook his head. "Beer comin' up on the right," he said, "and ya better wipe off your face if ya don't want some jerk-off lieutenant writin' ya up for desecratin' government property!"

"Bet I can beat 'em at tick-tack-toe," said Cow, who pulled a rag from under the seat and found a spot clean enough to wipe off his face. By the time he was done, Willy had driven the truck into the compound at Phu Bi and pulled into line for the night. They were halfway to the DMZ.

A large metal bumblebee sat on top of a tall pole in front of the Phu Bi gatehouse. Painted yellow and black, it wore a sailor's hat and carried the requisite tools and machine gun like a good Seabee should. Cow sat on a running board of the truck watching the dulled red sun come up through the heavy haze of another hot, humid day. His camera was ready and he had kicked bare a spot in the camp road where, in a few minutes, the Seabee would line up against the rose-colored sun. He had already checked the engine oil, tire pressure and the bottle of Aristocrat Brandy under the seat. Like the fuel tank, the bottle was a little over half full and he checked the cap to be sure it was tight. Satisfied, he wrapped it in yesterday's face-wiping rag before carefully putting it back.

"Look what I found," said Willy, carrying a small dirty Styrofoam cooler without a cover. "This was all they had in the mess hall, but the ice will keep the Cokes cool for at least a couple hours. One of those rags under the seat could cover it."

"Just a minute," said Cow, as he got up and stationed himself over his mark on the road. "Been waitin' for this. Probably the only thing in this whole damn place worth lookin' at." He pressed the shutter button on the small Fujica half-frame and then advanced the film with the lever on top. A second shot was for insurance. Advancing the film again, he turned and took a picture of Willy standing in front of the dump truck holding the little coverless cooler.

"Maybe we can send a picture to the Master Chief to let him know that 'war is hell!'"

"Oh, he already knows that," said Cow. "Why do you think he sent us on this safari?"

The convoy formed like it had the day before with the trucks rolling out of the front gate, one behind the other, only to stop on the right side of the road and wait. They were pointing north again and remnants of blacktop marked the middle of the road while sand covered the rest. Willy sat behind the wheel and Cow dozed with his cap pulled down over his eyes. His head was tilted back with his right arm draped on the top edge of the door. The other arm hung loose between the seats. He was nursing a hangover from too many beers in Phu Bi's EM Club.

Two more hours passed before the engines started to come alive in front of them and Willy pushed the starter button. "DMZ, here we come," he said, putting the truck in low and slowly letting out the clutch. "The sweeper must be makin' good time this morning. How'd you like to ride in that thing?"

"Bet they get a bang out of it," said Cow, lifting his head to check the cooler between them. "How about a cold one?" he asked and pulled off the rag on top. The ice was gone but its memory clung to the tepid cans as they each took one.

The mountains were behind them and the road here was straight and flat. As the convoy picked up speed, another great snake of dust grew with it and crawled all the way to the city of Hue. A small sign on a three-foot stick marked the "Hue City Limits" and Cow thought it was a joke because the sign was in English and the tallest thing for blocks around. Whatever had been there before was gone and only debris remained. "God," he said, "they sure leveled this place—there isn't a piece bigger than a brick."

Willy kept his eyes on the road as it curved to the left and some buildings came into view. He was taking in as much as he could—the shredded tops of trees and gouged trunks—

glassless windows and yawning doorways—two and three story buildings with bullet holes in every square foot of their stucco walls.

"Key-riest," said Cow, "look at that!" A huge white statue of Jesus Christ with arms spread split the road ahead. Behind the statue, a cathedral lay between the lanes and the trucks veered to one side or the other.

"Must be a miracle," said Willy, "but I don't see any bullet holes in it. How in hell can that be?"

"Beats me," said Cow, hanging out over the door trying to get a picture.

Moving at little more than a walking pace, Willy asked, "Notice anything missing?"

"Ya, a little hooch in this Coke."

"No, I mean people. There's only been a couple since the sign: a mama-san in black pajamas and a pointy-hatted papa-san with a long scraggly beard. Better keep that 16 handy."

Beyond the buildings, a tall overgrown berm blocked everything else from view. In places, the overgrowth was blown away where shells had landed and large craters pocked the slope. Still, they saw no more people.

"Kind of spooky," said Cow, making sure he had a round loaded and locked in his M-16. He kept the rifle in his hands and rode that way until they were well north of the city.

An arid stretch followed and they nearly reached thirty mph before coming to another abrupt halt. When they stopped, they could hear the pop, pop, pop of rifle fire and Cow took his M-16 off safety. Willy brought his up from the floor where it had ridden in front of the seat and pulled the bolt back. Sliding it forward, he pushed a shell into the chamber and waited too.

Truck engines were turned off up and down the line and the convoy noise collapsed in the otherwise quiet countryside. From their seats, they watched as the firing continued forward and far to the right. The shooting seemed to be coming from a squad of infantry moving toward two thatched huts, a half-mile from the road. The actual target could not be determined, but a cloud of white smoke soon began to rise over the huts. At first, it was only smoke but tall orange flames quickly swept up the sides and through the straw roofs. In less than a minute, there was nothing but walls of fire. Thirty seconds after that, the walls collapsed and only the white smoke remained. The show was over.

"It's like they were never there," said Cow.

"No, I guess they weren't," said Willy.

"Think someone actually shot at us or they just wanted to take out those huts?"

"I don't know. It would be pretty foolish to take a pot-shot at a couple miles of trucks and artillery in broad daylight."

"Maybe it was just a weenie roast."

"That's what I was thinkin', but there ain't a marshmallow in sight."

Cow reached under the seat again for the brandy. It was something of a ritual now, a poke in the eye of the military.

Willy was about to take a drink when Cow said, "Under the seat," and Willy immediately complied.

A lieutenant was walking down the middle of the road glancing at each truck as he passed. "Hit?" he asked, when he went by.

"No Sir," said Willy, and the officer kept going while Cow chuckled under his breath.

"Shot at and missed, SIR, shit at and hit," he said in a soft sarcastic voice when the officer was beyond hearing. "Ya know, this must be one of the dumbest fucking things I've ever done. How come they're shooting at us and we're shooting at them? They ain't got a pot to piss in or a window to throw it out. Not even a straw hut to put a window in. And we're here trying to stop the spread of communism? They don't even know how to fucking spell it! How long do you think it took to build those huts? I'll bet it was a lot longer than it took to burn 'em down. Maybe that's why they're mad at us. They ain't got shit. Maybe if we quit burning their houses and rice paddies we could get somewhere. What do you think?"

"I think you're gettin' drunk, again" said Willy, who started the engine and shifted into gear.

"Don't you ever ask yourself what the hell you're doing here with bullets flyin' around your ass? I sure as hell have and I don't like the answers. Did you ever start to add up the enemy KIA's from *The Stars and Stripes*? I swear there can't be that many people in all of North and South Vietnam put together. And they expect us to believe that bullshit? I mean, is this worth fighting and dying for? The best road in the whole fucking country is a strip of tar with so much sand on top that you think you're driving through a desert. The only thing I really know is that we can't stop the spread of communism here because there ain't no self-respecting communist who would ever be caught dead here."

Willy just listened and drove on.

"And here's the good news, Bucko—just when we think we're done with this shit in a couple months, they're going to take us home and turn us right around for another tour. How do you like them apples? Sometimes I think that when I go home I'm going to keep right on goin' north until I'm across the border."

"What are you going to do then, visit the queen?"

"Nah, but I gather that a lot of guys are. Going north, that is. But I also hear that the Canucks don't like us much more than these gooks. God, ya just can't win!"

Willy parked in the line next to the truck he had followed into a large sand field. When Cow's window was next to its driver, the Marine looked over and asked, "Ya got any more of that stuff ya been drinkin'? Been watchin' in the mirror and sure could use a taste."

Cow brought up the bottle. It had an inch or so left and he took a swig before offering it to Willy who waved it away.

The Marine's arm met the bottle half way and almost jerked it out of Cow's hand. "All urine," said Cow, as the Marine hoisted the bottle and the liquor began draining down his throat. When the bottle was empty, Cow nodded toward the back of the truck and the Marine tossed it up and over the side to where it landed in the box with a shattering crash.

"Now I wonder how in the hell that ever got there?" mocked Cow as he and the Marine climbed out and began talking. Willy set the emergency brake, left the keys in the ignition and got out with his rifle and backpack.

Cow came around to Willy's side of the truck, "Says there's a chopper coming for a ride back to Da Nang if we need a hitch. Should be here in an hour or so on the other side of those shell casings. Says to be ready when the bird drops 'cause he won't wait long—jump on and get the hell out of Dodge. Said 'Thanks!' for the hooch too."

The same lieutenant who had walked by on the road came past again. "Leave the keys in the ignition," he said. "We'll reassign the truck in a few minutes," and kept going.

"So much for appreciation—thanks for bringing it up here—nice of you to let us use it—sorry for the inconvenience! Let's get the hell out of here," said Cow, and he took his rifle but left anything else in the truck. "Traveling light this afternoon," he added for clarification and began walking toward the landing zone. "Guess whoever gets the keys can clean it up."

They were skirting the casings stacked to ten feet when Willy stopped. "There must be a couple acres of these things. How'd you like to have been on the receiving end of all that shit?"

"No thanks," said Cow, "but I guess that's why they call it 'no man's' land. Stand next to that stack like a ruler and I'll get it on film."

"Yeth-thir, Mither Director!" mouthed Willy who moved over to the stack and gave Cow the finger as the picture was taken.

"I'll get ya a copy for your girlfriend," said Cow putting away the Fujica. "It's the real you!"

The LZ was a bare piece of ground on the west side of the casings and five men were already lounging around waiting for a ride. Cow was still considering the casings and trying to understand how that many shells could be fired, how many guns it would take and for how long.

"This where we catch the chopper?" asked Willy, and a chorus of grunts affirmed it.

One guy said, "It should be here in twenty-five minutes or so; they're usually close during the day—otherwise it'd be anybody's guess. But he won't be shuttin' down those blades when the wheels hit so you better be jumpin' on or it'll be tomorrow before you get another chance."

Cow looked at the guy's worn fatigues and the scoped, smooth-barreled rifle. "Goin' south?" he asked.

"Gonna drop down to Da Nang for a week or two and then maybe head south." He picked up Cow's gaze at the rifle and said, "Can hit a quarter at five hundred. Basically, it's an M-14 but it's been worked over a little. Quite a little, actually. Here, take a look." He handed the rifle to Cow who brought it up to his shoulder and peered through the scope northward into the DMZ.

As far as he could see, there was nothing but a prairie of tall tan grass, limp in the afternoon heat. "Nice piece," he said, as he handed it back to the sniper.

"A little early, but I think I hear him comin'. Better get ready." In one fluid motion, the sniper stood with the rifle clamped to the end of his arm as if it had grown there. "Been three weeks," he said, "can sure use a beer."

"Come on," said Willy to Cow, "we got a date in Da Nang. And the Master Chief is probably missing us."

"The Master Chief probably don't even know we're gone 'cause he'd put a hold on that chopper if he did!"

The Chinook came in high and dropped down abruptly. Its twin rotators cut the air above their heads as the seven men ran crouched under the blades into the open rear end. There was no door, no end gate, not even a net across the opening, and, as soon as the last man jumped in, the door gunner in front gave a thumbs-up to the pilot who pushed the throttles to the max for liftoff.

The gunner yelled as loud as he could over the engine noise, "Hang on tight!" as the rear of the chopper came up first. Inside, Cow could see the maneuver in his mind like every other helicopter he had watched take off. Leveling for only a second, the front end then pointed upward and everyone clung to the netting and lines along the wall.

The Chinook climbed steeply to get out of rifle and rocket range. With his fingers tight in the webbing, Willy nodded his head toward the rear and Cow's eyes followed his direction. The land below was framed squarely by the opening and the countryside took on the washed, faded hues of an old map: light greens against pale sand and pale sand next to gray-blue water. Minutes later, further out and away from land, the seawater was dark blue as they followed the coast south.

The flight only took forty minutes and they were back to where they had started. "How's that for service?" asked Willy as they stepped out of the Chinook onto the tarmac of MAG 16. The heat came through their boots immediately and they could see the sniper's tracks in the tar as he walked away with his rifle shouldered.

"Just like always," said Cow. "Right back to where we started from—only we don't pass Go and don't collect two hundred bucks—God, I hate this place!"

"That's the trouble with you," said Willy. "You're always looking on the dark side. Me, I always try to find the bright side. By the time we walk through that gate across the road, the EM Club is going to be open and I'll bet a half-dozen cold beers have 'Willy' written all over them. Come on slacker, let's pick up the pace, that beer ain't gonna get drunk by itself."

VIII

Red Beach

In a narrow haze, the carrier floated between flat white water and a low overcast white sky. On the new tarmac, Cow and R.P. sat in the tire truck counting the fighter jets lifting off, ropes of exhaust trailing behind. Periodically, when the haze thickened at sea level, the ship seemed to be covered by a white scrim until the dark ropes of the skyward planes lifted the veil again. In the clearing, the gray man-of-war would reappear—deus ex machina.

It was midmorning and if any sound from the distant jets cut through the mist, the sand of Red Beach soaked it up leaving a nervous, deathly silence. In the tire truck, it was quiet too with concentration floating in and out of the passing minutes but a tire still needed to be changed.

Cow had driven over the tarmac very slowly looking for the earthmover. The Euclid TS-24 was even bigger than most of the helicopters that would use the facility when it was finished, but the scraper was nowhere in sight when they stopped. In the back of the truck, the new tire, over six feet in diameter, hung loosely from a crane pivoting slowly in eighth turns, back and forth, left and right, like time unwinding.

"Ten," said R.P., barely raising his voice.

"Yeah," answered Cow, watching another black line being pulled into the sky. "North?" he asked, and R.P.

nodded. Cow started the motor remembering again that the guard at the gate said it was safe and a minesweeper had swept everything—but that had been said before.

Berms lay at the north end of the tarmac like foothills to the mountain range behind them. R.P. pointed in their direction and said, "It has to be out there."

Listing in the sand, the nose of the yellow scraper began to protrude from the end of the line of berms as they got closer to the end of the metal matting where Cow stopped the truck. "What a son-of-a-bitch this is going to be," he said, getting out and slamming the door behind him.

The driver of the Euclid sat in its seat waiting. "Cut it," he said when they got close. "Just come out of the hole and didn't see the post. Don't know what it was doing there but drove it into the bottom of the tire and out the side. Thought I could still get unloaded but couldn't, so here I sit."

Cow kicked the sand with his boot: "How the hell are we going to put a jack on this shit?"

"We can't," said R.P. "She probably weighs 50 ton. We'll have to shore her up and dig out below."

"Christ," said Cow, "what a deal."

"Just didn't see that little metal post," said the driver. "But I can get all the equipment we need and there's plenty of timber out by the road."

Cow and R.P. stared at the tire only half-listening.

"Come on down and come with us," said Cow. "We'll get some of that lumber and then you can find a crawler to do the digging. We'll need to pull the truck back here too so we can reach the tire with the air hose."

The driver of the earthmover sat between Cow and R.P. "See that gate way over there?" he said, pointing across the tarmac. "It's just to the right of there where we filled in the ditch and tore out the bridge. But watch out, there's still a lot of sharp crap where it came down."

"Down?" said Cow and R.P. together.

"Where the shit hit the fan," the driver said. "There's still a lot of small crap they missed in the cleanup. Can't blame 'em though, was a sorry mess. I didn't see it go up, but sure as hell heard it. Lucky no one else was killed by all that shrapnel. Some of it came down way on the other side of those berms back there. Must be a good half mile."

"I heard it was a five-hundred pounder," said R.P. "How the hell they get it in here?"

"Probably planted it back when we first started and there wasn't much security. I don't know, but it sure was a mess and we drove all over this area when we were working around here. They never knew what hit 'em. There was hardly enough left to put in the bags. I got here in a couple minutes but it was hard to figure out at first what happened. There was just this big hole and nothing else. I think the biggest piece of the jeep was a pound and a half, and looked like it came from the starter or generator. Landed back where the Euc is now."

"Jesus," said Cow. They had all heard about the two men—a young engineering officer and a builder who had come along to check on the site.

"What's the chance there's another one?" asked R.P.

"Oh, I doubt it," said the driver. "They were all over this place after it happened. Covered every square foot. Of course, we drove everywhere around here before it happened too."

The lumber had been neatly stacked so the explosive rain was on the inside. On the outside, it looked almost new. Turned over, the burgundy stains told the story as it was loaded.

Getting back in the cab, the windshield was wet from drizzle moving inland and Cow turned on the wipers. Returning to the Euclid, they crossed the tarmac for the third time and the carrier came back into focus still floating between heaven and earth. It was alone now with no black lines tying it to the sky.

"Any snipers around," Cow asked the driver between them.

"Big sniper out there the other day," said the driver, casually pointing toward the carrier. "The New Jersey fired on-and-off for a couple hours. When I shut down the Euc, you could hear the shells going over, wooozshhh, wooozshhh, wooozshhh, like they're drilling through the air. Heard they can drop those things into a sand box thirty miles away."

"Halfway from here to Laos," said Cow. "But I don't know where that is. Sometimes I don't even know where here is."

"As long as I ain't in the sandbox," said R.P. opening his door as they came to a stop.

The three men carried the lumber to the Euclid and laid it lengthwise and crosswise on the sand before stacking the short blocking beneath the frame. Hydraulic jacks tightened everything and when the whole machine sat solid, the driver left to get a crawler to dig out under the tire.

While he was gone, a hydraulic bead breaker was clamped on and pumped by hand to loosen the tire from the rim. Pushing the tire wall inward, they used a maul to tap back the locking ring that formed the outer edge of the rim and took it off. After removing the ring, the bead breaker was placed on the back of the rim to loosen that side of the tire. The rubber clung to the steel until the top of the tubeless tire was pushed outward and expanded beyond the outer edge of the wheel to hang open from the inside. Only the heavy bottom tread remained pinched between the wheel and the sand.

The crawler made tracks in the sand that followed it from the distance until the driver pivoted the machine in front of the wheel with one side pulling forward and the other back. Repeatedly, he filled the bucket and backed out creating a ramp in the sand that left the whole tire hanging loose on the rim above. At last, with little space to spare, he slid the bucket under the flat tire and lifted it slightly before inching backward and taking it away.

It was precarious work. No one trusted the blocking or the sand on which the earthmover rested. The work had to be done cautiously and carefully—bombs, snipers and warships out of mind—but nearby. The crawler carried the new tire from the back of the truck and replacement of the locking ring followed. An inflation band forced the beads against the edges of the rim and trapped the rushing air from a long red hose stretched back to the truck's compressor.

"Twenty-two pounds," said R.P. pulling his tire gauge away and capping the valve. Cow began to roll up the air hose as the driver on the crawler pushed sand down the ramp to fill in around the now floating tire. On semi-solid footing, the jacks were pulled out and the driver climbed up onto the Euclid to start both the front and rear diesels. Raising the pan, still fully loaded, he pushed down on the throttle and both engines roared. The four huge tires churned up the sand together, climbed over the shoring and carried the driver away under another unraveling rope of exhaust.

By midafternoon, the morning mist had given way to sun and puffy clouds. Behind them, in the truck's mirrors, the carrier now floated on a blue sea under a mostly blue sky. The big ship seemed farther out and smaller with only its tower visible above the flight deck which was nearly down to the water line. If the sea got rough, the whole ship would disappear over the horizon.

Cow drove extra carefully, calculatingly slow, toward the gate where they had to unload the blood stained lumber. "What were the names of those two guys in the jeep?" asked R.P., but neither remembered for sure because they were in another company and it was already old news.

IX

Chicken Fingers

The China Beach USO had a liquor store, reading room, game room, and space for in country R&R. It also had a real café, telephones to call home if there was an open booth and a guest book—though the definition of "guest" was loosely interpreted. As if especially invited, soldiers passing through signed the book and looked over the list of previous signers to make connections with someone they might know from their own state or hometown. Despite the incongruity, it was nice to know you were not alone.

Cow stopped at the liquor store at least once a week with extra ration cards, more often if he could come up with needs or excuses to leave camp with the tire truck. At China Beach, he always checked the book on the way in because he would have his hands full on the way out. First, he looked down the states' column to see if Wisconsin had been scribbled in, then for any town near his home, and, finally, at the scrawled names to see if he knew who had come through. He seldom found anybody, but kept looking and always signed again to stay current and near the front of the book. Each time he came in, he would scan the pages back to his name from the time before and then flip forward again to the beginning.

Cow was not looking for anyone special, just someone who could lend a moment of reality to the peculiarity of being in Vietnam: someone to say, "Hey, I know you; you're from Hillton and were a year ahead of me—or behind—in high school." Someone to share the reality of neighbors, girls, cars, beer bars and all the little idiosyncrasies that spoke to belonging somewhere, anywhere other than where they were.

The sign-in was an exercise that said, "See, I'm not the only one here," even if the signer was usually standing there alone. In ten months, Cow saw only two names he had recognized. One of them, Stephen Craig, was a small kid who he remembered from grade school and had not seen since. He knew he was the right guy, however, from the hometown inscribed and by the small circle above the "i" in Craig's last name. Cow took one look at that circle and was instantly transported back to the 8th grade. For some unrecalled reason, instead of a dot, Craig began to put a small circle above the "i" in his last name. It was a miniscule breech of practiced penmanship but rankled the 8th grade nun to no end. She wanted him to use a dot like everybody else and quit showing off.

The battle went on for nearly a week and Cow remembered the day a new touch was added. The "smiley face" had caught on and an amateur rendition floated above Stephen's last name at the top of his English paper. It was the crowning insult and the nun went into a tirade for nearly an hour until the closing bell ended her hoarse discourse. They had a substitute teacher the next day because the sister had lost her voice; and by the end of that day, nearly every kid in the classroom with an "i" in their name, and some that did not, had a smiley face drawn above it. The nun had lost the battle and the war.

The shopping list taken to the USO was always the same: whiskey, brandy, vodka, and as much beer as could be concealed in the cabinets of the tire truck while still getting through the camp's front gate. The ration cards used to buy the booze and beer were supposed to control the amount of liquor anyone could purchase and, presumably, it worked. But since the cards were not identified by owner, they could also be shared and were. The more cards you had the more you could get for yourself and your buddies.

Cow and R.P. stopped at the USO on the way back from another tire run. They had quickly changed the flat leaving plenty of time for procurement. The objective was to fill the truck's empty cabinets and be back on base before lunch and mail call. Cow was looking for a care package from home and it was overdue. From a preceding letter, he knew it contained cookies, cake, and newspapers for wrapping. Letters from home did not provide all of the news, especially parts that were not pretty, but the newspapers used for packing generally told the stories, intended or not.

When a care package arrived, Cow, like the others, shared it at the end of the day with the rest of the guys in his hooch. Most of the time, the food disappeared nearly as fast as it was unwrapped. This time, however, it seemed to go even faster because Cow kept smoothing out the newspapers and putting them in order. Finally, he had to grab for the last chocolate chip cookie and piece of cake or be left out of his own treat.

The wrapping du jour was almost always the **Hillton Herald** and from the crushed and wrinkled pages Cow followed the twists and turns of life at home without him. He found the names of old girlfriends who had gotten married and it made him feel left out and empty. He also read of babies born, traffic forfeitures, farming accidents and deaths from around the area, though he seldom recognized any of the names in the obituaries. He did not have to go to the obits though for the bold front-page news that read: **Local Soldier Killed in Vietnam**. That bold-faced type stood out even in the poor light of the hut with everyone standing around, cake and cookies in hand, crumbs falling to the floor.

The dateline said, *Wilmer:* and then, *Private Stephen Craig lost his life in Vietnam while on patrol northwest of Da Nang according to a spokesman with the Department of the Army. Stephen's parents, John and Judy Craig of rural Fox Junction, were notified of his death this past week. Stephen was an Army infantryman serving in Vietnam's northern I Corp with the 3rd Infantry Brigade....*

72

Cow said aloud to anyone listening, "You know the guy I told you about with the smiley face that pissed off the nun?" and he began reading from the *Herald*. The words came out of his mouth but his mind was churning through their youths. He wondered how Stephen Craig had found his way into the Army. He had not asked that question when he found his name in the book, but now he remembered again that Stephen Craig was a little guy, not very coordinated, and always the last one to be picked for any grade school baseball game. Last, that is, until his secret weapon was discovered and then he was always first because his hands and fingers were so small that he could get chicken fingers on the top of the bat for first-ups when nobody else could.

Cow still saw the light in Craig's eyes every time he won that last grab of the handle with five little pinkies perched on top. As a result, Stephen Craig became the MVP of the 8th grade year because recesses were short and if you did not get up to bat first, you probably did not get up at all. Baseball and the 8th grade, odd things to think about here and now, thought Cow. Then he said aloud again to no one in particular, "How do you figure? How do kids in elementary school get from baseball games to here and never back to bat again?"

That evening, after Cow and a couple others went down to the shop to empty the tire truck of the beer and booze, he also wondered if Stephen Craig was one of the guys marching along Highway 1 when he and Willy passed them with the convoy going north to the DMZ. He remembered the poor bastards humping their packs over the mountains, up and down the dirt road, one step at a time, while hundreds of trucks passed them by and even chicken fingers would not help to get a ride.

Two days later, on another tire run and stop at the USO, Stephen Craig's name was still in the book, only a few pages further back. The shopping list waited again as Cow flipped through. When his survey was finished, he looked over both shoulders and seeing that no one was paying any attention to him, pulled on the corner of the page with Stephen's name on it, ripping it sharply and cleanly from the spine of the book. Folded in half, twice, he pushed it into his shirt pocket thinking he would send it to Stephen's parents.

Soon, however, Cow's resolve to send a letter and the memento became tangled in the realities of Vietnam where there was no baseball, chicken fingers, smiley faces or 8th grade MVPs. The daily business of being in Vietnam was consuming and his intention to write retreated to somewhere behind his own front line. After all, he began to reason, he only knew him from grade school and that was a long time ago. Moreover, he did not know the parents at all and would be writing from a place they were probably trying to forget. And what could he say, he asked himself, to make it any better anyway?

X

Incoming

Marine Air Group 16 was the target because it had spotter planes, choppers, pilots and guns. It also had one mile of asphalt runway between Highway 1 and the South China Sea with Marble Mountain on the south end. The mountain marked the end of East Da Nang and stood like a gravestone protruding three hundred feet above the sand.

The mountain was an impressive piece of rock, but except as a sniper roost and runway dead-end, it had no real effect on operations. The small reconnaissance planes lifted off in a very short distance and the helicopters did not need a runway at all. As a result, by design, experience and security, aircraft and personnel were concentrated on the north end of the airstrip away from small arms targeting and directly across the road from the military hospital.

The Seabee base camp was between the hospital and Marble Mountain on the west side of the road. From its rear perimeter, the basin formed by the Han and Vu Gia rivers stretched further westward all the way to the mountainous horizon. Security bunkers dotted the back line atop the edge of the sandbar created by the South China Sea when it formed East Da Nang ages ago. In a sharp slope down to the rice paddies and river line, the face of the sandbar was covered with concertina wire, lights and claymore mines.

Cow had been on security for six weeks. For the first thirty days, he had been on the day shift to get the lay of the land, but now spent nights in bunker eleven. Eleven was the midpoint of the west perimeter and he shared watches there with J.J., Johnny Jax. Like other bunkers, the two men took four-hour turns with two shifts one night and one the next unless there was action. If something was stirring they were both expected to be on duty and fully alert.

A little after midnight, two weeks into the rotation, Cow was scanning the basin with the Nite-Vision Scope when he spotted two people moving toward him. Carrying what looked like a pole or tube when he first saw them, they were at least a thousand yards to the southwest. Without taking his eye away from the scope or off the target, he called to J.J. resting below, "There's movement out there, you better get up here."

Thirty seconds later, J.J. crawled up the ladder onto the observation deck, rubbed his eyes and lifted the binoculars from the ceiling hook. He tried to look out but quickly put them back unable to cut through the darkness with the standard optics. Straining his eyes, he looked over the river into the black grass beyond, "Where?" he asked.

Cow pulled back from the scope on the plywood counter and slid over to make room. "Just beyond the board-walk, where the trail comes down from that little bridge. Looks to be two of 'em."

J.J. put his eye to the scope and slowly moved the lens over the area until he saw them, "Yeah, I've got 'em, looks like two gooks and a mortar. Call it in."

Cow already had the transceiver in hand and pushed the button that connected them to the base central command bunker. He waited a few seconds for a pickup and when someone answered, pressed the talk button: "Bunker eleven. We've got two unidentifieds carrying what appears to be a mortar at two, four, zero degrees and approximately one thousand yards. Requesting permission to open fire when they are within range." He lifted his finger from the button and waited for the reply he knew was coming.

"Permission denied. Continue to monitor while we check for any patrols in the area. Repeat, permission denied."

Cow did not recognize the voice but hung up to relay the message to J.J. who had moved back from the scope and was now hunched over the Browning Automatic Rifle in front of him. "Hold on," Cow said. "No go on the permission. They're probably checking on patrols in the area. I suppose there could be an ambush set up out there somewhere."

"Patrols, my ass," said J.J. with his thumb on the safety and finger on the trigger. "I can see them coming right down the trail and they'll be setting up that mortar in another minute or two. How far you think now, seven fifty?"

"Yeah," Cow said, "I've got them in the scope. Definitely a mortar and two gooks. Let me try again."

"Bunker eleven," he said after connecting. "We have two gooks and a mortar at two, four, zero degrees, estimated seven hundred yards and closing. Request permission to open fire."

He waited for what seemed to be an overly long pause before the unknown voice came back again: "Permission denied, repeat, permission denied. We are checking on patrols in the area and have not received an all clear. They could be our guys. We're going up the ladder."

Cow continued holding the transceiver in his hand. "No dice," he said to J.J.

"Jesus, they can't be much more than five hundred yards!" and J.J. kept the rifle on target while Cow nudged the scope slightly to keep pace with the movement.

"They've stopped," Cow said. "You'd think they'd at least hit the warning siren. Maybe they think we're full of shit." He pushed the button once more and waited several seconds for a response. "Bunker eleven," he said, "they're setting up the mortar at five hundred yards—correction, they have fired a round! We've got incoming, I repeat, INCOMING, request permission to open fire! Here comes another one."

"PERMISSION DENIED, REPEAT PERMISSION DENIED! We can't risk it. We're waiting on this end too! Repeat again, permission denied!"

"God-damn it," said Cow, as he heard the thuds of the mortar rounds exploding behind him. Sirens began to wail from MAG 16 and their own siren followed as three more rounds quickly chased the first two.

J.J. was counting the flashes from the mortar tube and listening to the rounds whistle as they went over. "Four, five—five—five, six. Christ, how many did they carry? Seven," he said at last as the rumble of exploding shells echoed back from the target diagonally behind them.

The phone in Cow's hand squawked in his ear and the voice on the line barked: "Confirm the yards, five hundred?"

"YES!" yelled Cow, "REQUEST PERMISSION TO FIRE!"

"Hold your fire, we haven't received permission from on top—we had to go up eight levels and it has to come back down from the airbase, I can't authorize it for Christ's sake! Where are they at again?"

"Two, Four, Zero degrees and five hundred yards!"

"Sons-a-bitches!" said J.J. That last one was short and they're folding up! Come on, who the hell is asleep up there? The bastards are going to get away clean!"

"Keep 'em in your sights," Cow said as he pushed the talk button once more: "Are you still on line? OK. They're moving out, request permission to fire."

"Permission denied, repeat, permission denied! We should know in a minute, just hang tight."

Cow held the phone with cramping fingers and J.J. clung to the BAR as the distance expanded. Sirens continued wailing and men who had been rousted from sleep came running from their hooches with their M-16s to man the open sandbagged pits on the security line.

J.J. said, "I can barely see them."

Cow kept his eye tight against the scope. "They're almost to the foot bridge again, nine hundred yards and a lot of tall grass out there. Almost where I picked 'em up. Look at 'em run—di-di-mou—they're really haulin' ass! I won't even see 'em with this scope in a few seconds."

Cow was holding the scope with one hand and the transceiver to his ear with the other. The voice came back at last: "You may commence firing, repeat, you may commence firing."

"THEY'RE FUCKING GONE!" Cow screamed back. "THEY'RE FUCKING GONE!" and the line went dead.

At breakfast, word was that a mortar shell hit the hospital intake area and killed two corpsmen. With his mouth full, J.J. said, "I knew that last one was a short sons-a-bitch."

Cow thought the eggs were a little watery, but the bacon was crisp as usual even if it was cool on his plate. It was nearly seven and they were the last to come in and eat. Things were often on the cool side before they got to it.

XI

Five

Two weeks remained on Cow's security calendar and it was a welcome change to be back on days. Days were less demanding and he liked the light. He was still in bunker eleven, but alone now because of experience and spent the twelve-hour shifts on the back line looking west. Nothing was happening close in, but farther out, if the sky was clear, he often saw jets on strafing runs and the billowing smoke after their bombs dropped. Sometimes, the orange explosions were so large that they could be seen even from a distance of fifteen or twenty miles. When the wind was right, he could also hear the blasts a minute or so later.

The BAR sat on its tripod to his left with the cartridge belt snaking down to an ammunition box on the floor. The Nite-Vision scope was to his right, unneeded, and his M-16 leaned against the sandbags behind him. The magazine was full and inserted, but nothing was chambered. On most days, even the transceiver gathered dust between calls on the quarter hour.

Since the end of the spring rains, the sun had gathered strength causing the afternoon heat to grow under Cow's hardhat and flak jacket. It was uncomfortable, but they were mandatory and he could not set them aside even if his head itched terribly and his undershirt was soaked. Besides, there was no point in arguing with himself or anybody else. Rules were rules and orders were orders.

Except for the heat and fighting in the distance, little changed from hour to hour or day to day. The concertina wire and mines in front did not move, nor did the landmarks in his field of vision. At the bottom of the sandbank, the patchwork of rice paddies changed color at a snail's pace or not at all. Fifty yards beyond, the blue-gray river lay flat and smooth under the sun and clouds.

A half-mile to the north, a small island divided the river where a single defoliated tree stood sentry somewhere near the middle. When he used the tree like a gun sight, Cow could pinpoint the Da Nang runway five or six miles away and watch the F-4 Phantoms leap into the sky. In the heat of the afternoons, the horizon shimmered and camouflaged the takeoffs until the jets broke through in full flight. Wheels up, the pilots would stand the airplanes on their tails at full throttle and rocket into the sky. At the top of each climb, still under full power, the nose of the airplane would rotate downward until nearly level and the whole thing would disappear into the distance. Like their namesake, the appearing and disappearing was almost instantaneous.

To the left of the bunker, beyond the wire and not far from where the perimeter made a right angle turn to the rear, a small grove of bent palm and banana trees enclosed a spring that streamed out into the river. The fresh water served a small village a hundred yards further south and out of view.

However, during the day, while the village boys worked in the rice paddies or tended the water buffalo, the women and girls came down to the spring to get water, wash clothes, and sometimes bathe. Cow had heard stories about the bathing beauties, but from bunker eleven all he ever saw was the curtain of trees.

One very bright and hot afternoon, after the water buffalo had been taken back to cool in the shade and almost all other movement had ceased, only the heat waves danced above the island until the sound of helicopters broke the lull. From his left, Cow counted five Sikorskys coming in low over the river past the trees and spring. The thumping sound from each of their rotors nearly melded into one as they came forward in a straight line. They were old olive-drab ARVN copters and it was evident that they were playing a game or showing off. One after another, following the leader, they touched the water with their wheels, one side to the next. Side-to-side, wheel to wheel, they came forward tilting left and right like waddling ducks walking on water: one, right—two, left—three, right—four, left....

Four helicopters passed in front of him, but the fifth chopper was a little further back and slightly out-of-sync. That pilot may have been the new guy learning the tricks of the trade or maybe he had been distracted and was trying to catch up. No doubt, it took masterful flying and a lot of practice at upwards of a hundred miles per hour. And practicing may have been the idea as the first four shot by with long slices in the water that left centerlines for the last one to follow.

Timid perhaps, the last chopper did not rock nearly as much as the others did. Perhaps the pilot needed a little more attitude, altitude or daring. Whatever it was—missing, off kilter or unaccounted for—just before passing Cow's post both of the helicopter's front wheels simultaneously bit into the river with catastrophic results. The resistance of the water instantly pushed back against the tires and the nose of the aircraft pitched forward. When the nose dropped, the long top rotor blades sliced into the water and shattered while the tail rotor somersaulted over the cabin. For an instant, Cow had a snapshot of the pilot looking at him from the window, strapped in his seat, upside down, as the helicopter came apart around him. In that fraction of a second, even the window disintegrated when the cabin exploded in a maelstrom of debris that continued pushing forward and downward into the river.

Only three or four seconds elapsed from the time the two wheels touched the surface until the final pieces of the helicopter were under it. After that, only the river remained with water rings moving outward from the spot where the helicopter went in. Cow instinctively reached for the transceiver, but stopped. What would he say to central command? There was nothing in front of him and the first

84

four choppers had flown away, presumably duck walking down the river.

As the sound of the departing rotors faded, the water rings washed to shore and the river leveled again as if nothing happened. None of the choppers came back and there was nothing left to be seen. "Yes," Cow said to himself, "there were five and now there are four. At least that's what I think I saw."

It was unfathomable. There was no wreckage. No one swam to shore and nothing floated. With binoculars, Cow scanned the river closely but only the heat waves kept moving in the middle of the hot afternoon. There were no telltale marks in the water and no clue as to where the first four helicopters had gone: left, right, or over the island. There was not as much as an oil sheen on the water.

Pushing up his hardhat to let out some of the heat, Cow rubbed his forehead before turning toward the curtain of trees. Two young women were standing where the stream emptied into the river. They appeared to be looking at the spot in the water where the helicopter had gone down and held up towels or clothing in front of themselves. One of them pointed and shook her head with moving lips but no sound reached Cow's ears. Turning then, both walked back upstream on thin stick-like legs that seemed to go all the way past their naked bony hips up to their sharp jutting shoulders. It was a fleeting sight, and, with a few steps, they were covered by the trees as before.

No bubbles rose in the river and there were no helicopters to be seen or heard. Where the two young women had stood, only trees and heat waves remained. Cow opened his flak jacket and thought that maybe if you were in the air, over the river, passing the stream—maybe then a window would open and frame two skinny naked girls bathing on a hot afternoon. It was an image he held in his head juxtaposed to a mosaic of mistake and shattered glass.

XII

Calico

Bunker nine faced a military junkyard on the south side of the perimeter. Lights and coils of concertina marked the separation but there was never enough light, especially in the middle of the night. Filtered and diffracted through the curls of wire, the light only seemed to supplement the ghostly hazes and fogs that caused the junkyard to eerily shimmer and shake, disappear and reassemble.

The two-story bunker had the usual sandbagged walls and roof to protect from shrapnel and gunfire. At ground level was a small single room with a door to the rear and a cot along the wall. Above, the requisite BAR sat on its tripod capable of sweeping 160 degrees if needed and a ladder in back linked everything all the way to the roof. On top, lumpy sandbags covered the plywood and often made a bed when nighttime lows were still in the upper 80s.

From sunset to sunrise, two men took turns staring at the junk and shadows in front of them. The shadows were the kicker because they often appeared as solid as the objects that made them. They also changed on any given night or hour because of flares, landing lights and the moon, or lack thereof, until which was what became scrambled and uncertain. As a result, even if the junk did not move, the shadows usually did, changing, crawling and creeping through the night watches.

Nearly everyone who ever spent a shift in No. 9 swore there was movement out front and the logbook was rife with such reports. In the morning, some guys just laughed it off on the way to chow. In the middle of the night, however, there was no laughing when the whole yard seemed to be coming alive with motion and movement.

Cow's ninety days on security were officially over, but not actually. His Temporary Duty Assignment was simple and it moved him to the ninth bunker because he was needed and available. Experience counted for everything and nothing in those decisions as no other explanation was necessary. He did not know how long he was going to be there, but the word was that his TDA would be another seven to ten days—or nights.

The nights had been hot and the roof remained the coolest spot for sleep, especially if there was any breeze because the small room below acted like an oven where the sandbags roasted in the sun all day and oozed heat all night. Besides, Cow always thought, the chance of a mortar round landing on one little particular piece of roof was at least somewhat improbable, chance being what it was.

It was also dark and there were no railings on top, so Cow carefully laid his M-16 to the side before stretching his double-folded blanket over the smoothest lumps in the middle. His helmet went next to the rifle and he rolled his flak jacket into a pillow. Lying on his back, he stared into the sky, eyes and face tight from squinting into the junkyard trying to see into the metal. By contrast, the night sky was soothing in its black beauty and easy familiarity. He had nearly four hours for the muscles in his face to relax.

On a clear night, the top of the bunker was a quick transport home where the same constellations crossed over and carried the observer back and forth. Cow found Orion's belt and almost immediately fell into a deep summer's sleep and a picnic back home. He was lying on his back there too, only in an alfalfa field beyond the parked cars. Then, like now, he was looking up into the black polka dot sky while Katie stripped off leaves from the alfalfa stems and dropped them on top of him. She was being playful even though he was still too bashful and shy to really see or understand her.

Under the stars and on top of the field of canvas bags beneath him, Katie now sat next to him tossing leaves that smelled like new mown hay before giving way to her coconut perfume. She leaned over, kissed him, and he touched that place on his face before pulling her down on top of him. He could feel the warmth of her weight on his chest and the press of her thighs on his. While they kissed, his fingers slipped through her hair, now his own, and the kisses magnified his yearning in a dream where the stars remained bright over her shoulder, even if his eyes were closed.

In his head, he could see all of her from above while below his fingers opened her blouse and undid her bra. Behind his eyes and in front of him, her pink nipples stood in the cooling night air atop the white mounds that he dreamed of touching. He was still kissing her, looking at her and moving with her as his hand found where her jeans should have been, but were not. Over the round curve of her hip, his fingers followed the warm fissures between the sandbags.

Both absolutely real and positively imaginary, she was with him until he was pulled by hand onto his shoulder and side. The hand, guiding and firm, came out of nowhere and stopped him a half-second from being in her complete embrace. In that moment, the field, stars and Katie disappeared as though sucked into a black hole inside his name. "Cow!" said a breathy voice accompanying the hand pulling and pushing on his shoulder. "Cow, wake up. It's time for your shift. Come on, tell me you're awake and I'll go back down and wait for you. It's ten to 2:00 and I'll make the report before you take over. Are you awake?" Cow nodded his head with his eyes open, the wind-driven smells of new-cut forage and coconut still teasing his nostrils. His right hand rested, palm down, on the round warm side of a sand bag as he tried to find in the night sky where the field and Katie had gone.

He had to get up and get going, but in an instant was back to sleep again searching for Katie in the field behind the cars. When he found her, she pressed against him and his hand followed her hip while she caressed his face with her mouth locked to his. Her coconut perfume grew even stronger as the sounds of a picnic carousel and shooting gallery closed in on them until, just before reaching the pinnacle of her charms, his name ricocheted through the night with a roaring burst from the BAR below.

"Cow! Get down here...." And by the "Get..." he was already sitting up straight reaching for his helmet and flak jacket. The Browning sputtered again and Cow could see far enough over the roof as he went down the ladder to watch a tracer veer off into the night sky after hitting metal in the junkyard.

The transceiver's red light was already blinking as Cow ducked his head through the low doorway. His partner, shoulder to the rifle, was squinting down its sights with curls of white smoke rolling from the end of the barrel like ghosts being let out of a bottle.

"What's out there?" Cow asked.

"When I came back down they were just pulling back but I got a shot at 'em."

"How many?"

"I think there were three that I could see. One's eyes were so bright that he seemed to be looking right through me."

"Were they in the wire?

"No, I don't think so. Out between the trucks."

"Jesus," Cow said, picking up the phone. The green light glowed next to the red one when he pushed the talk button. "Bunker nine reporting a possible breach of the wire," he said, looking at his watch, "at approximately 1:58. There is no current enemy fire and no other confirmation."

Cow listened for a moment longer. "Yes, Sir," he said, "I will relay the message and stand by for further instructions." He hung the phone on its hook and said, "They want us both on duty for at least the next hour."

"Shit!" was the only reply Cow heard before continuing. "The OD is coming over. He'll probably want to know what all the shooting's about." Cow was looking at the rusty rear rims of a burned-out truck fifty yards away. There was no door on the cab, no hood, and the dump box was twisted from the force of the mine it must have hit. The remnant of a jeep, shoved into and under the rear of the truck, was almost buried beneath the overhanging tailgate. Four ridges of sand lined the deep crawler tracks left from pushing the jeep into the pile.

Nothing moved and the light did not change until some clouds gathered and began to hide the moon. The shadows shifted then just as both men heard the steps of the officer coming toward the bunker. Cow led the password exchange with "Curious."

"George," came the reply and the ladder squeaked as the OD climbed up. Inside, he stood quietly between the two men looking out at the same detritus of war illuminated by the perimeter lighting. Under triple scrutiny, they stared at the piles of junk that may, or may not, have been moving.

Funny, Cow thought, I can still smell the coconut in the air and she's twelve thousand miles away. The wind continued to kick up from the southwest and the rings of concertina wire vibrated and shook in the gusts. In the junkyard, dust, dirt, leaves and palm fronds blew across the rutted sand where the crawler had pushed the jeep and metal carcasses leaving its rutted telltale trails. Two eyes glinted through the wind driven dirt from near the top of the nearest truck and Cow heard the safety on the BAR click off. At nearly the same time, he also saw an arm reach into his peripheral vision as the OD said, "Hold on," and laid his hand on the stock of the gun.

The first two bright eyes disappeared, but, almost as quickly, two more lit up just above the crawler ruts where the bright metal of a crushed C-ration can glinted. The can was the focal point and from the top of the truck, behind the jeep, and inside the rut, three calico cats emerged at nearly a full run toward the spilled lima beans and ham.

XIII

Craps

"Come-onnn seven," ricocheted off the concrete walls before slipping out of the casino. The concrete was hot and so was the game with five bare backs under a single 100w bulb.

The casino walls rose in the sand like Stonehenge slabs: flat, gray and incomprehensible. They were supposed to be the new showers, something of a testimonial and departing gift to the replacement battalion, but were never finished. Technically, the only thing really missing was the water; but without water, the walls only soaked up the sun and lent themselves to nighttime entertainment.

Above the beckoned seven, the bare bulb glowed from the end of a black cord draped over the inside wall. From there, the cord drooped across the changing room and disappeared into the darkness outside. Nearly unobservable, the cord then angled down and snaked its way across two hundred feet of sand to the camp generator where it had been surreptitiously plugged in after lights out.

Inside, the light cast shadows beneath the men kneeling in the sand. The wall in front of them served as the rail and the game board was a piece of plywood pushed tight against the concrete by the players' knees. On either end of the inside wall, openings connected to the changing room and from there to more sand and dirt outside. Except for a few muffled words of encouragement to the dice, and a very, very faint glow overheard, nothing left the confines of the casino except winners and losers.

The eagle had crapped earlier in the day and all of the players' pockets were full except for the bets on the board. The heat was on for Rondale Jackson and the walls blocked any breeze as he tossed the dice. The two cubes hit hard, bounced back onto the plywood in his coming out roll and stopped with a three and five on top. "Eight's the point," he said, studying the dice. "And my ten's down." Four more tens followed. Jackson needed seven to win, another eight to lose, and anything else to keep going. He was up a hundred and eighty in less than an hour.

"I'll raise the bet another ten," said Billy-Joe, and the other four had to follow or lose what was already on the board. Billy-Joe was down the most and he was trying to get some back.

Rondale tossed the dice again and they tumbled back with a three and a six.

"Craps," someone said, "shoot again."

Picking up the dice in his right hand, Rondale blew on them for luck. "Come-onnn seven," he said, a little loudly, and threw the dice hard against the wall.

Mark Turow, Lieutenant Junior Grade, was the officer of the day and inspecting the perimeter defense line.

He had been stopping at each bunker, checking for alertness and attention by giving the password and monitoring the reply. The night was quiet and the trek got him out of the command center where it was stifling and monotonous. Making the rounds on the dark moonless night, he also spent a few minutes in each bunker talking softly with the guards on duty.

Cow had the early watch in Bunker 9 overlooking the junkyard, and, when the Lieutenant came in, asked why the perimeter lights had blinked earlier? It was a curiosity he had noticed for some time.

"I don't know," said the Lieutenant, "this is the first I've heard of it."

"There's usually only one flicker and then they're steady again. I've seen it before and have been wondering about the generator. It's generally just after dark but I've seen it happen during the midnight watch too. Not every night, only every other night or so. It's like something's plugged in or turned off and the power dips and surges."

The Lieutenant repeated, "I don't know, but I'll check it out," and left the bunker. Once outside, Turow, a man of his word, altered course from the perimeter line toward the mid-camp generator station. He weaved between the dark huts of sleeping Seabees and came out into the open only a few yards away from the concrete shower walls. On the sand, his walk was nearly silent when he heard something that sounded like "Ates-da-point" and paused to listen. For a fraction of a second he did not hear anything more and was about to continue toward the generator when, "And my ten stays down." was very clear. He turned his head slowly trying to pinpoint the voices until he heard, "I'll raise the bet another ten," and a low rustling was followed by two almost inaudible clicks coming from inside the shower walls to his left.

There was no moon and the concrete was nearly black in the night as he sidestepped slowly with his hand out until he touched the wall. Standing still, "Craps, shoot again," and, "Come-onnn, seven!" rolled into his ears.

The Lieutenant's first inclination was to go in and break up the game, but a hesitation suggested not walking in alone even if he knew where to enter. Withdrawing his hand, he stepped forward in the direction of the command bunker several hundred yards away. A couple MPs would be there and they could come back with lights.

The Lieutenant had just begun to pick up his pace when his left foot snagged the black electric cord where it lifted from the sand and began its assent. At that moment, in nearly full stride with his upper body leaning forward over his right leg, his left foot followed the cord higher until the slack ran out and it became a trip wire. His momentum carried him forward with arms slashing through the air for support until he toppled face first into the sand and dirt. If anyone had been listening, "Oh, shit!" slipped past his lips as he went down.

The cord, caught on the Lieutenant's boot, came with him as he toppled. Inside the casino, pulled from outside, the light bulb shot upward until the socket caught on the sharp edge of the concrete above and the bulb exploded. Hot shards of glass rained down on the bare backs of the players below and "Whattttt-the-fuckkkkk?" emanated from five voices in the instant darkness.

Ten hands grabbed for the now unseen cash on the board and Rondale whispered, "Quiet, anybody got a light?"

The silence said no.

"Let's get the hell out of here," said Billy-Joe, but he was already too late and shoved against the wall by the others colliding in their grope for the openings.

Rondale was first into the changing room and poked his head outside cautiously until he could make out the Lieutenant squirming on the ground trying to get his foot free of the cord. Billy-Joe came up behind and bumped into him. "Other way, dufus!" snapped Rondale, pulling back and reversing direction.

The Lieutenant could hear the commotion inside and yelled from his horizontal post, "Halt, Stop!" But Rondale and Billy-Joe were already sprinting through the far opening, faintly outlined by the distant perimeter lighting. Following the first three men, they ran for the maze of huts and safety where, once inside, confidence and composure returned. In a minute or less, each gambler was lying in bed as if he had been there all along.

With his foot finally freed, the Lieutenant stood up just soon enough to make out the last muffled footfalls fade in the distance. He dusted himself off as best as he could and proceeded straight to the command bunker where he secured a flashlight amid inquisitive stares asking, "How in the hell did you get that dirty?"

Ignoring the stares and not asking for help, the Lieutenant went back out and retraced his steps to the showers. With the flashlight in hand, the cord was clearly visible hanging limply from the top of the wall to where his foot had caught it. He followed the cord to the generator and unplugged it; only this time, because of the broken bulb, there was no telltale flicker in the perimeter lighting.

Back at the shower, the Lieutenant looked for tracks before taking into account that everyone in the camp wore the same style boot. Inside, he shined the light around the first room and overhead at the black draped cord. The dark doorways at either end beckoned him into the casino where, on the plywood, shards of broken glass glittered like billboard lights on a Las Vegas night. The dice lay where they had landed with five points on one, two on the other; and three pieces of script, ten dollars each, nestled in the kneed hollows at the edge of the board. Picking up the dice and bills, the Lieutenant shoved them into his pocket to mix with the sand already there.

XIV

Pennsylvania 6-5000

Hank Williams was not a breakfast buddy, neither were Tammy Wynette, Loretta Lynn, or Dolly Parton. "God-damned hillbilly shit," is what Cow called it when he pulled his pillow down tight over his head. Like it or not, the music and men he bunked with were definitely from south of the Mason-Dixon Line. Good guys, all of them, but with impaired musical tastes—at least in his opinion in the morning.

"Hell," Cow routinely blasted, "reveille doesn't even go off until six, what have you got against sleep? It's five in the morning for Christ's sake!" Almost as often, on his way out to an extra early breakfast, he unloaded his disdain for the twangy sounds of Hank Williams by mimicking the high nasal falsetto: *"Your cheeeee-tin' heart, makes me weep, I try and try, to get more sleep; but sleep won't come, because of you, and your god-damn radio, ohhhh, fuck you...."* Sometimes a boot would hit the door as it closed behind him. Mostly, though, laughter and single-finger salutes rated his performance.

Armed Forces Radio began its Da Nang broadcast day at 5:00 a.m. with the national anthem. During the week, ***The Country Kickoff*** followed the anthem and it drove Cow under his pillow. He hated country music at that hour of the morning. Not that he disliked it all: "I think Johnny Cash is

101

good," he often said. "And Marty Robbins too. But not at five o'clock in the morning! *'Your cheeeee-tin' heart....'*"

Nearly all of the alarm clocks in the hut were set to go off at 5:00. On the weekends, however, there was always a frantic punching of "Off" buttons as ***The Country Kickoff*** was replaced by the big band sounds of the 1930s and '40s. On those mornings, the tables were turned along with the volume on Cow's radio. Blaring as loud as Hank, Tammy or Loretta did on any weekday morning, guys like Jimmy Dorsey, Guy Lombardo, Benny Goodman, and Lawrence Duchow held sway.

Cow knew a little about Lawrence Duchow but not much else about the music. That was because Duchow and his Red Raven Orchestra started out in a little town not far from Hillton where they played at the Red Raven Inn and appropriated the name. People still talked about him there and the reason he left for California. Some said it was a chance for the "big time," but others insisted there was more to it. Cow did not know if there was anything else to it, but, to the best of his knowledge, Duchow never came back home to Wisconsin. Not that it would make any difference to the hillbillies around him who now had their heads buried under blankets and pillows.

In time, Cow learned to pick out "In the Mood," the "Cherokee/Redskin Rhumba" and Duke Ellington's "Take the 'A' Train." After a couple of months of self-imposed attention to detail, some of the bandleader's names even began to help shape the musical mayhem.   In the twilight of the early weekend mornings, Cow would shout out, "Hey, guys, it's Gene Krupa!" or Dizzy Gillespie, Stan Kenton, Count Basie, or Woody Herman: anybody to twist the knife. With the name still rolling off his lips, he usually checked again that the volume on his radio was all the way to the top.

It was tit for tat, not unlike the rebel flag stapled to the rafters across the aisle. The flag over that bunk did not matter to Cow, but it did sum up the soldier lying beneath it with his head under the covers.   Five days to two, Cow thought, looking at the Stars and Bars.   The truth was that some wars take a long time to end and there it was again: North versus South, different battle but the same conflict.

Tommy Dorsey's "On the Sunny Side of the Street" was winding down as the DJ wound up, "This is your Armed Forces Radio Network in Da Nang, South Vietnam. It's five-seventeen in the morning and do you know where your sergeant is? No? Well, who cares anyway—but if you want to call home, we've got your number—here's Glenn Miller with *Pennsylvania 6-5000*." Cow wished he could call home but there were no telephones for that. The guys buried in their beds were probably wishing the same thing.

XV

Ringer

The ball-peen hammer hit the galvanized pipe to end the round and Slim dropped his gloved hands as he turned back to his corner. A chair was waiting there and he sat down with indifference. R.P. lifted a can of Coke to Slim's lips, toweled the wet forehead and wiped off the gloves. Draping the towel over his own shoulder, R.P. rechecked the gloves' laces, gave Slim another drink and stepped over the rope to get out of the way.

Hung from tie wire, the pipe rang again as the timekeeper started the second round. Slim, already on his feet, stepped away from the corner toward the center of the ring as a big Marine crossed the clay coming toward him. When the Marine was close, Slim's right foot shot outward in a feint and he pushed off to catch the square face solidly from the left. Slim was quick, very quick; and by the time his opponent realized he was being led, Slim was already around and behind him. Turning to follow, the big guy stepped into another blow to the head, stumbled and swung wildly at his retreating nemesis. In almost the same instant, Slim reversed again and quickly landed three more punches to the mid section.

The Marines thought they had the power and were willing to pit their big man against all comers. Slim, on the other hand, was a ringer and sleeper in the common parlance.

At first glance, you did not notice the smooth bulging biceps, the length of his arms or the size of his hands. Least of all, you did not pick up on how fast he moved and with how much grace. Steps were not steps as much as glides and slides off the balls of his feet and the tips of his toes.

Initially, it did not appear to be a fair fight because the Marine was obviously a heavyweight. Slim, a little under one eighty, was at least one class below, though each time the pipe rang it became clearer that the underdog was a match and more.

Slim sometimes talked about being a black kid who had to learn to take care of himself. He often said that he did not have much talent, but paid attention to detail and worked hard to get better at boxing. "Hard and steady," he said. "You have to be strong to strike, but it really is all in the legs. It's hard to hit a moving target and to keep moving you have to stay on your feet. It's something you have to learn and learn so well that when you're dog tired and can't think, your feet can do your thinking for you." By the time he was twenty, he was the local light-heavyweight champion and almost everyone knew enough to keep their hands off him. Almost everyone, that is, except his draft board. And, since he was no match for them, when the Army infantry loomed ahead, he joined the Navy instead.

Benny Beecher and a Marine nicknamed Booker held the bets, keeping track of them in two little notebooks. The Marines were gung ho and willing to put down two, three, and four to one on their big guy to win. The Seabee crowd did just as well taking the bets because there was no doubt in their minds who was going to come out on top.

Halfway through the second round, the Marine was still trying to box Slim into a corner although it was not working. Just when he thought he had him, Slim would slide by in the final millisecond with another series of kidney punches before backing away in anticipation of the next attack. Sweat was dripping off both of them, but it was particularly bad for the big guy who kept trying to wipe it out of his eyes. Slim's black skin glistened as if he had been rubbed with oil and the only punch really to hit him slid off his wet right shoulder. Arching back, he returned the strike with another left uppercut before wheeling around and dancing away.

With the hammer's fourth tap, Slim dropped his guard again and backed into his corner. R.P. was there with the towel and Coke. "He won't go another half round," he said, as Slim nodded in agreement while tapping the Coke can for another drink. "If ya get one more good hit and he stumbles, go in for the kill. Ya hear?" Slim nodded and kept his eyes on the opposite corner where the Marine was being wiped down. He had his right glove off to handle his own drink and Slim watched the manager slide the hand into the glove, tie it tight and put the mouthpiece back in. Both were ready when the pipe sounded for the third round.

The Marine got up slowly but then moved quickly to the center as Slim approached with caution. Both men had their hands up jabbing at each other as they circled looking for a way in. Slim had the longer reach but the big guy was reacting faster than he had in the first two rounds. Now, he deflected the thrusts and unexpectedly planted a foot between Slim's. Pushing forward, he was almost chest-to-chest and caught Slim's head solidly three times while the Marines yelled in unison from beyond the rope, "How do you like us now?"

Slim went down but caught himself with outstretched arms. The referee, who had stayed on the side up to now, began to come forward but stepped back when Slim came up quickly to get back into the fight. With his head high and eyes locked on his target, he resumed punching from just beyond the Marine's reach. Slim was still much quicker and the adrenalin shown moments before appeared to be draining from the Marine as his jabs and feet slowed. He was still very dangerous, but déjà vu set in as Slim had the sensation of being back in his biggest fight where he could sense the crowd, the bright lights and three ropes marking the edge of the ring instead of one. He also felt a few punches but now knew that he was the tougher of the two and would win. Just a little longer, he thought, tire him a little more: step back, close in and keep your hands up. Left, left—left, right—all swirled in his head as he kept floating on his feet jabbing and swinging. The big guy poked and punched, but Slim dodged or deflected most of the blows while countering with hits to the stomach, sides and back.

Slower still and more unsteady, the Marine took one last wide swing and Slim stepped forward from behind the arc. Closer than he had been, another hard left uppercut to the jaw preceded a roundhouse right to the side of the head. The Marine lifted with the first punch and jerked to his right with the slam of the second. His knees buckled and he dropped in a twisting motion that put him down with one glove tucked under his chest and the other splayed out to the side.

Slim watched him fall with both of his gloves held just a little higher. Still light on his legs, he turned to his corner with two jabs at the air as the pipe rang. Behind him, the referee kept counting, "…and six, and seven, and eight."

XVI

Jungle Boots

The EM Club opened at 5:30 with a waiting line outside. R.P. and Benny Beecher were already there when Cow joined them and reached into his shirt pocket for an envelope. He fished out the letter with two fingers and began reading aloud through watering eyes and bursts of laughter. Most of the guys in the line listened and stood looking down at their new jungle boots with incredulity written on their faces. Even after a week-and-a-half's wear, the leather toes and heels were still black against dark, unbleached, camouflaged uppers. Compared to their original heavy leather boots, these were soft, light, and cool in the heat. They were also difficult for Seabees to come by.

When Cow looked up from his overly dramatic reading, at least a dozen faces smirked back at him. All were wearing the new boots and understood the simple answer as to where they came from. If asked, the basic truth was, "A passing jarhead traded them for some directions."

A little later, after the first beers of the afternoon began to wipe away the heat of the day, some new guys came up to ask if there were any more boots available. The word was out, but Cow had to say no because all of the extras were gone. Benny and R.P. did not say a thing with the letter still tugging at their cheeks in the form of silly grins.

The letter was high praise for the men of the tire shop who generally did not get much attention and were mostly thought of as deserving less. Addressed to Cow and signed by the Company Commander, the letter cited attention to detail and excellent care of government property. In particular, it congratulated him and the men of the tire shop on their initiative while pointing out the "newly painted" tire changing machine adorning the shop floor. The machine did indeed look newly painted. In fact, it was new paint and the metal underneath was new too. But that detail did not come up because it was not mentioned by anyone assigned to the area—the least of whom now wore new jungle boots.

Nearly a third of "A" company had been shod as the tire crew amassed a multitude of future favors in exchange. The boots had arrived on the back of a Marine deuce and a half, six pairs at a time for ten straight days. On each of those mornings, the truck was driven into the battalion compound and backed into the tire shop for attention. When the driver, a corporal, got out and stood back to watch, the rear wheels were jacked up and the tires given a cursory once-over. At the same time, another tenth of the old tire changing machine was dropped into the truck box and twelve new boots lifted out. The swap complete, the jack was lowered, mock salutes exchanged and the truck driven away.

The corporal, from the Marine Air Group across the highway, had been bringing flats to the tire shop for months. One day he ventured, perhaps a little out of sorts for having to

112

rely on others or cope with the inconvenience, "I sure wish we could get our hands on a tire changing machine. It would save everyone a lot of time and trouble."

Cow said, "I think that's possible. What could we trade?" Looking down in thought, the Marine focused on Cow's heavy black boots and struck upon an idea that he thought he could swing with his supply guy.

"Let me check it out," he said, "but I think I could get my hands on some jungle boots if you'd be interested."

Cow was interested because his feet were always hot in the sweated leather; and, after the corporal left, he climbed a narrow shaky stairway in the far back corner of the shop that led up to a storage deck in the rafter trusses. A new tire changing machine had been left up there by the previous battalion. It was in a wooden crate that Cow had found one lazy afternoon while reconnoitering in the attic. From all appearances, it had been placed up there with a crane, perhaps while the shop was being built. Later, it was apparently left behind as forgotten, unneeded or ignored.

By the time he came down, Cow had a plan to fix the unbroken machine on the shop floor just like Johnny Cash built his Cadillac *One Piece At A Time*. With R.P. and Benny helping, the three men cautiously disassembled the upstairs machine and brought down a few new pieces each morning after muster. Late in the afternoon, the corresponding parts were removed from the old machine and replaced with the new. The old pieces were then placed on the workbench at the back of the shop where they were unnoticeable among the hammers, bars and assorted tools of the tire trade. In a drawer beneath, the directions from the new machine awaited the last delivery.

The new tire changing machine was a real beauty with bright paint and no scars or worn parts to hinder its operation. The color alone made it stand out among the dull and dirty tires leaning against the shop walls. It certainly drew attention, and, when the Company Commander brought in his jeep with a leaking tire, even he stopped to stare at the little jewel in the middle of the floor. The three men watched, first with anticipation that the ruse was up, but then with relief when the Commander moved on. More than just a little under the gun, the jeep's leaking tire was dismounted, repaired and replaced so quickly that its driver had barely made it up to his office before being told that it was ready to go again. This further impressed the Company Commander and resulted in the letter in Cow's pocket.

It was a good deal all around. The Marines were happy to have a tire changing machine; the new boots looked and felt good; the Company Commander was proud of his outfit; and, because the two machines worked so well, the tire crew had less work to do and more time not to do it.

XVII

Animal Cookies

The new CO might have been from Berkley instead of Annapolis or he brought a little of his own hometown fervor with him.   It is also possible that he was just an Animals fan and liked the humor of it even if his age might suggest otherwise. Whichever, on the morning after he took command, reveille went off with a completely new beat. At breakfast, it was all the talk with speculation that whoever pulled the prank was going to have a very bad day. When the next morning began the same way, however, ears and attitudes perked up.

At five in the morning, five miles from the DMZ, the standard blown bugle notes gave way to what was on every mind and not even Beethoven could think of rolling over for another five minutes or forty winks when the day started with this:

> *We gotta get out of this place*
> *If it's the last thing we ever do*
> *We gotta to get out of this place*
> *'Cause girl, there's a better life*
> *For me and you.*
>
> (*The Animals*)

Jobs did not change, the mortar attacks did not stop and the days did not get any cooler. Yet there was a change in the air that made things simpler and, as every short-timer crossed off another day, clearer that the upper echelon finally understood what any E-3 could easily have told them.

XVIII

Thirty-Three

"Cody," said R.P, "I'd drop that if I was you."

"And I'd do it right now!" added Cow.

Cody was standing in front of them with his right arm extended. In his fingers, he held a four-inch spike by the point so that the head end kept a small green snake from falling off. The snake hung neatly over the steel, draped half-and-half on either side. Lime-green, it was as big around as a pencil and did not squirm or twist, though it might have.

Small, lithe, and twice as long as the spike, the snake apparently did not find Cody's fingers to be adequate forage or a threat. Cow and R.P. on the other hand, did not think it wise to wait and see if it changed its mind. "Cody," said Cow, and Cody lifted his head slightly in acknowledgement. "Cody, I don't think you quite understand. What you are doing right now is flirting with death and that is its instrument." Cody furrowed his brow slightly as he hunched his shoulders. They were gestures of questioning, mistrust and defiance while he peered at his prize dangling just beyond his fingertips.

Benny Beecher came up and stepped between Cow and R.P. "What gives?" he asked, placing a hand on each of their shoulders. Both men nodded toward Cody who was still studying the little creature riding the spike like a twig of bamboo. With one look, Benny said, "Cody, these guys aren't messing with you now. What you have at the end of that nail is a genuine bamboo pit viper and if it latches onto your fingers you are going to be a dead man before we can call for help."

Cody did not sense the danger and had no trust either. He had joined "A" Company right out of boot camp, only ten days before, and the little green snake certainly looked harmless enough. Maybe, he thought, if they are so damned worried about it, he ought to toss it to them and see if they could catch it. Cody was going to be very cautious about anything they told him because his new hat was still chafing.

On Sunday afternoon, three days before, Cody had stopped writing a letter home to step out of his hut into the beer and baloney of the late afternoon. Most of the guys knew he would come out eventually and, when he did, they were ready to greet him. "Throw a couple bucks in the pot and have a beer," someone yelled. Cody dug into his pocket and tossed two crinkled bills into a hat sitting next to a cutoff barrel filled with water, ice and cans of cold beer.

He was shy and looked around uneasily at the assemblage of shirtless Seabees in cutoffs and caps. Nearly all of them were drinking beer in the hot afternoon. A few even tossed around a football one-handed, a can of beer in the other. Not really knowing any of them, he sat down on the edge of the porch and looked on quietly.

After a few minutes, Benny Beecher stood up with an Olympia in hand and pulled a machete from a crack in the decking. Checking it over, he ran a finger along its edge to test for sharpness. A sawhorse with a new center plank stood nearby and he brought the machete down hard into the wood. "Who's got a buck to bet they're the best?" he shouted, and the footballers stopped long enough to give him a glance. They knew the drill.

"I'll find a blindfold," said R.P. and he returned a moment later with a green strip of cloth torn from a shirt. "Who's got the pot?" he asked, and Benny nodded toward Cow who was already collecting.

Benny said, "I'll lead off," tossing his hat onto the deck while taking hold of the machete, still upright on top of the sawhorse. R.P. put the blindfold over Benny's eyes and said, "Take your mark." Levering out the machete, Benny raised it and came down hard on the cross member.

"Don't move and I'll mark it," said R.P., drawing a line along the edge of the metal as the starting point. "Remember," he said, "you only get five hacks and I'll count 'em off. Ready?" Benny nodded. "OK, begin."

Benny again pushed down on the handle and lifted the machete free. Raising it high, he brought it down to the count of one. Four more times he pulled out the blade and chopped into the wood before removing his blindfold to see how he had done.

R.P. marked each cut and measured between the two outermost marks. "Three-and-a-quarter inches," he said loudly, "not bad, but probably won't stand. Who's next?"

Marris stepped up. "Buck's in," he said, and handed his hat to R.P. who tossed it onto the deck where Benny's had been. With the blindfold tied, a beer in one hand and the machete in the other, he was ready. Nearly everyone was ready.

When Marris pulled off the blindfold, R.P. measured the marked cuts. "A hair under two-and-a-half," he said, "steady as she goes and you're the man to beat. Buck a chance; come on, winner take all!"

McDoogle got up from the porch and stepped to the horse. He took off his hat and gave it to Benny for safekeeping. Tall, with a long nose, a little crack of light below his eyes let him see the horse when he had the blindfold on. With his mark set, however, he swung wide on almost every chop playing his part to the hilt.

"Four-and-a-quarter," shouted R.P. after the fifth hack. He was caught up in the excitement. "Not even in the running, remember, winner takes all and the pot is growing!"

Cody watched, sipping his beer and working up the courage to join in. He was, after all, the new guy and did not want to appear overanxious. The football players had taken a break and gathered around the sawhorse where they made side bets to help grease the wheel. The wheel was rolling well and by the time Cody gave Cow his dollar, everything was set and everyone was ready. Everyone except Cody.

R.P. motioned for a new sawhorse with a clean beam and began the stunt like a circus barker. "Step aside, step aside; let the new man show us how it's done." With the blindfold in one hand and the machete in the other, he motioned for Cody to come forward. "Ever use one of these before?"

"No."

"But you saw how we do it, right?"

"Yeah."

"Then I'll just take your cap and put on the blindfold," he said, handing the machete to Cody and the cap to Benny.

With Cody blindfolded, Benny tucked the back of the cap into the front and rolled the bill tightly. When he released his hands, the bill and hat looked like a slice of green melon or a small saddle destined to rest on the back of the sawhorse.

Cody took his first chop and R.P. said, "Hold it while I mark." From the other end of the sawhorse, Benny slid the cap along the plank and up against the machete. It clung perfectly, curled evenly over both sides.

"Ready?"

Cody pried the machete from the wood and raised it overhead for his first chop. As the machete went up, a last nudge pushed the cap directly beneath. R.P. said, "Begin," and when the machete came down it sliced cleanly through the hat into the wood.

The circle of Seabees who had gathered around let out a collective, "Oooooh," as R.P. counted one.

On the count of two, they added "Aaaahhh" and "Yaaahhh" followed three.

"That-a-way!" somebody yelled, "Two more and you'll take home the prize!" With that, the laughter started until even Cody began to catch on. Ripping off the blindfold, he found his hat sliced, diced and pinned to the wood by the machete.

Cody stood there taking it all in: the hat, the sawhorse and the laughter. A can of cold beer was held out in front of him as an offering but he would have none of it. "Bastards," he said, "who's gonna pay for my hat?" and with that, turned and marched directly back into his hut.

The laughter stopped for a moment as Cody walked away in anger and a few middle fingers flared behind him. "Joke 'em if he can't take a whatchamacallit!" came from somewhere in the back causing the laughter to start again. It had been a great performance!

Moments later, however, Cody came back out with a new cap and an apparent attitude adjustment. With some bravado, he doffed the cap in the general direction of the sawhorse and the men still standing around. His face was red but the heat may also have caused him to emerge in need of another cold beer. R.P. intercepted him on the way to the barrel and stuffed the pooled money into his shirt pocket. "Get yourself a new cap," he said, "and a couple cases of beer for next Sunday wouldn't be a bad idea either. Talk to Cow."

"Cody," Cow said, "I believe that what you have dangling near the end of your fingers is referred to as a '33' snake. That means, Cody, you get three steps or three seconds from the time it bites you until you're dead. I wouldn't test it, Cody. I'd just drop it."

Cody looked at the three serious faces in front of him sensing that this was not a repeat of the hat trick. At least it did not feel that way and just as the little snake began to twist its head upward in a one-sided, elongated "J," he dropped the spike. Three held breaths were expelled in unison as the little creature got its bearings on the ground and crawled away into some grass to get out of the sun. Cody followed it with his eyes but let it go its way.

XIX

Rodeo

Six fingers from each of the judges kept Benny in the running. It was the first time the judges all agreed and the satisfaction was apparent on their faces. Apparent, that is, until some of those fingers were needed to keep control of the beer cans grasped between their pinkies and thumbs.

The rodeo was a fast-paced program and the chute handlers were already getting anxious as Willie climbed on the barrel and Benny got up brushing off the sand. Settled down, Willie pulled the cinch rope tight and pounded down his fingers like he saw every bull rider ever do—all of them on TV. He also needed sixes or better to make the finals.

With his cap on tight, Willie nodded and the lines were pulled hard to set the steel bull in motion. Starting out, Willie shot straight up, dropped down, and twisted to the right. His free hand waved above his head as he snapped back to the left and his legs clamped tighter around the barrel. There was no raking of heels against the bull's tough metal shoulders; Willie was just hanging on to stay on. Whipped back and forth, up and down, all he could process in the short interval was the "...Thousand three, thousand four, thousand five..." counted out by the beer-drinking cowboys hanging on the fence. To avoid confusion, everyone on the fence line was a cowboy and everyone was drinking.

"Hang in there, Willie!" someone shouted, but the cinch rope slipped from his grip and he was bucked off the barrel.

Face down in the sand with the bill of his cap plastered against his forehead, he heard "...thousand eight!" and knew there was no need to look up for numbers.

Old telephone poles marked the corners of the arena. Each pole stood twelve feet tall and sixteen feet from the next. Pulleys were attached to the tops and four heavy lines ran to holes cut into the shoulders and rump of a fifty-five gallon drum. The lines, in turn, led to the chute handlers who were the four biggest "horses" in Alpha Company. Together, they pulled the lines, tossed off the riders and laughed about doing it while downing another beer.

Five judges sat on a bench to one side. Each had been bribed to do the job: first with beer; then with a place to sit instead of standing; and, finally, with more beer from the riders. Everyone understood the judges could be bought and the first thing a thrown rider did was head to the EM Club to buy more beer to enhance his score on the next go-around. The real cowboys bought the judges a beer before their first go-around.

Either way, the beers kept coming and the judges had their hands full. In order to give a score at the end of a ride they eventually had to set down the cans or hold them between their knees. This worked for the first several rounds, but the more they drank the more lax they became until a few digits held above the top of a can was the top of their ambition. As a result, threes became the rule.

A wooden snow fence had been set up around the arena to give the riders a little extra room and keep the fence line cowboys out. It also added some shade to the backs of the judges and helped keep their beers a couple degrees cooler. The riders' beer, on the other hand, kept getting warmer and the more they drank the hotter the cowboys became. With at least a dozen cans in each of their britches, inhibitions for buckin' bulls and anything else flew off like a rider with a slipped grip.

Like almost any good wild-west show, the scorer, announcer and general rodeo manager was from Montana. His name was Pete and he went by the sobriquet of Repeat, just like the joke, having earned the nickname because he said almost everything twice. Sometimes he just said the same word in succession, but at other times repeated a whole sentence like an echo of the first. It was not a stutter, more like being stuck while he looked around for what was to come next or back at him. In the interval, being unable to keep his mouth shut, the second words just followed the first. It was like being on a road trip with someone who reads billboards aloud as you pass by. You both see the same thing but everything that goes into the other guy's eyeballs dribbles out of his mouth. The only difference with Repeat was that what he said was what he heard himself say.

Between beers, Repeat was busy writing down points, calling up riders and mimicking a real rodeo announcer. And each time another head hit the sand he did his best to ease the pain. "Aw, heck—aw, heck—let's give him a hand—give him a hand!" He meant well and certainly did not mean to add insult to injury—but the beer took care of that.

With the sun heating up the barrel, behinds began to be scorched and tempers started to flare. The first real evidence of discontent was a thrown rider's fistful of sand aimed at Repeat. It missed him, but pinged off the beer cans held by the judges who took a sober view of the intent. When another rider soon pulled the same stunt, the judges, who did not like sand in their beer, called for an automatic deduction of all points except one—the one given with their middle fingers—which resulted in two more fistfuls of sand flying at all of them. Reacting as usual, Repeat let out a "Shit—shit," before trying to duck out of the way and spilling beer all over his score sheet. Angrily, he whipped the clipboard holding the wet paper at the retreating rider who was trying to crawl out from under the bouncing barrel. The clipboard missed him, but Repeat caught the guy by the legs and dragged him back to the middle before swinging wildly with his Montana fists.

The four big horses on the lines stepped forward and tried grabbing Repeat to pull him off. But Repeat swung at them too until they began to swing back and the five judges had to jump in to help set things straight. That made eleven

Seabees flailing at each other until a few would-be cowboys leaped the fence and joined in too.

Because the chute handlers had let go of their lines, the barrel was in the center of the melee. Bulging fists slammed into the steel while the ropes slipped down from the pulleys and tangled the writhing limbs in heavy hemp. The rest of the spectators, still held back by the snow fence, cheered for whoever was on top and tossed beer on everyone else. Soon, the whole pile looked as if it had been dipped in egg, rolled in crackers and was ready to be deep-fried in the humid heat of the hot afternoon.

Repeat finally saw daylight and crawled out. Rolling up against the snow fence, he gasped for air between exclamations of, "Jesus, Jesus," and "some-bitch, some-bitch!" The errant cowboy was next out and pulled himself up with the help of the fence. Darkening bruises already discolored his face and his knuckles were skinned from banging against the barrel. Unfortunately, he still had a rope wound around one ankle and when someone tried to toss the barrel out of the arena, it pulled him back down into the sand for another go-around.

Eventually, though, the beer, sun and sand came out on top. One-by-one, the punch drunks peeled off and headed back to their huts with bloodied noses, various cuts and contusions. By the time security arrived, everyone was gone and the only things left to see were the banged up barrel, a tangle of ropes snaking around the arena and four pulleys atop the poles like vultures eyeing the aluminum empties below.

Later, Repeat said, "That's—that's the way of the rodeo—the way of the rodeo." He had a broken nose and tooth marks on one ear. The tooth marks came from someone he called the "Rabid rider—rider."

At the dispensary, the medic who put him on antibiotics said it was, "Just in case. Just in case."

XX

Griesedieck

Hollis was from St. Louis and liked what he called "Gree-zee-dick." Joseph (Papa Joe) Griesedieck may not have liked to hear his name pronounced the way Hollis did it; but, like it or not, after founding the Falstaff Corporation in 1920, a lot of suds went down thirsty throats with his surname floating on it. The name was, of course, a localism held together by reverence, ridicule, crudity and nostalgia—all plentiful in Vietnam.

The hut where Hollis slept was a plywood shack shared with 15 others. Like all the rest, it sat on four-by-fours buried in the sand and had a metal roof with screened eaves to let in some of the breeze. The overhang and screening kept out most of the rain and bugs—but not completely. To dampen the effects of shrapnel and keep the metal roofs from rattling when low-flying jets screamed over, sandbags were laid on top. On sunny days, the sacks of sand looked like brown potatoes on a galvanized frying pan. On rainy days, nobody looked up.

Sandbags also surrounded the outside walls nearly to the eaves of the huts to stop enemy fire, and the bags gave a certain mass to the thin construction of the buildings that belied their actual strength and potential longevity. In a shallow bow to architecture, narrow porches graced both ends

131

with the gable roofs extended to cover them. Depending on the day, the porches were a good place to get out of the sun or rain, write a letter or drink a beer. A porch light was about the only thing missing.

Hollis was from a long line of men who worked at the Falstaff brewery keeping the bottles full and sliding down the line to their two-fisted connoisseurs. He said his father was an electrician and some of that savvy apparently rubbed off because Hollis was not afraid of a little jolt now and then. As a result, whenever some illicit wiring in the hut was needed, he was the designated operative.

Like a treasured keepsake, one of Hollis's most prized possessions in Vietnam was a Falstaff beer sign. Where it actually came from was a bit of a mystery but the China Beech USO was a strong possibility. The fact that it lit up and turned, a half world away from St. Louis, also added immensely to his enthusiasm. The sign's only defect was that the cord did not have a plug, but that was simply overcome by pushing the bare wires into the slots of a receptacle.

Initially, the sign hung from a rafter above Hollis's bunk and he inserted the two bare wires whenever he needed it for light, ambiance or reminiscence. If he forgot to pull out the wires whenever he left, it made no difference because it was a welcome sight when he returned. Like so many little things, it was a first-rate, secondhand connection to home.

Sunday afternoons were free time for most of the battalion and a spirit of company camaraderie ensued. In preparation, a stash of beer and booze was brought in via the tire truck during the week. Additionally, on Sunday morning, the wrecker was used to make a run to MAG 16 for ice, and, sometime before noon, two or three guys would raid the chow hall for the main entrée. Wood was gathered from wherever it could be found to make a fire in a cut-off fifty-five gallon barrel. The outdoor cooker sat on a pipe tripod with a top grate cut from the steel radiator grill of a Euclid earthmover. At a suggested cost of nearly seven hundred fifty dollars each, the radiator grill was considered a bargain when only half was needed to cover one barrel and two cookers could be made for the price of one.

Great ideas simply flowed on Sunday afternoons, especially by the time the sun was going down and all of the full bottles neared empty. On the previous Sunday, late in the day, a suggestion was made to bring out the Falstaff sign so everyone could see it and have a little light added to the evening. Being proud of his heritage, hometown and beer, Hollis jumped at the idea to keep the party going. By midweek, still pleased with the result, he hung the beer sign permanently from the gable above his porch. A few screws into the roof sheeting held it tight and a small slice in the screening allowed the cord to be fished back inside to the receptacle.

For the next few days, the sign oversaw the comings and goings of Hollis and his squad. Lit each evening, and sometimes early in the morning, its turning light greeted inhabitants and visitors to the hut. It was proving so popular that on Saturday night Hollis hard wired the line into the receptacle even though he did not have a switch. "It's as well left on as off," he said and nobody gave it a second thought.

Steaks were on the menu in the chow hall the next day and a couple dozen were appropriated. Later, they sizzled on the grill until every piece was gone, washed down by the beer and booze that tempered another week in country. As the week and the day slid away, it was nearly dusk when the first thuds of incoming mortars registered on the weekend revelers. A moment later, the sound of the MAG 16 sirens came up as the men scrambled for their rifles, flak jackets, helmets and bunkers.

The mortar attack did not last long and the target, as usual, was the Marine Air Group helicopter base across the road. On the other hand, the time required to reestablish a secure condition was lengthy and it was well after dark before the situation was resolved and the all clear given. At night, when conditions warranted, "lights out" was an order—and mortar attacks certainly met those conditions. When the mortars started falling, very few lights, if any, had been turned on. The exception, to the chagrin of Hollis and his foxhole inhabitants, was the lonely white Falstaff parallelogram turning progressively brighter and brighter as the daylight turned to darkness.

From an advertising perspective, "Papa Joe" could not have asked for more! From a security perspective, however, the light presented a problem and a target. As a result, well before the all clear was given, the Falstaff light suddenly went out and what remained of it was later found lying in the sand. The severed cord was readily identifiable but the rest of the fixture had been smashed to smithereens.

Hollis fumed nearly all week vowing to find out who had wrecked his sign and mocked his hometown, its prized beer, family and relation. By the next hot, sultry, Sunday afternoon, however, with his hand wrapped around his tenth cold can of Falstaff, the beauty of the sign resurrected itself in his way of thinking. A revolving beacon in the darkness of the lights-out night, its memory spoke volumes about who was there, what they were doing and where they were going. He drank to that, talked of home and laughed about the revolving white light well into the dark of night.

XXI

Camouflage

According to Shiell, the new wrecker was a Christmas gift. "A little something from the Department on the Fence," he liked to say. "Nothing like a '67 Mustang or Camaro: but it's the sport model with a drop top, seating for two and a slick stick shift." He was obviously proud of it and when not hooked to roadside wreckage or loading pallets with the boom, used the extra time to wipe off the dirt, wash the windows and blacken the tires with a little diesel fuel.

One Sunday afternoon, instead of drinking beer and horsing around, Shiell jacked up each wheel and painted a narrow silver band on the metal rims just inside the tire bead. The result of the detailing, according to a few observers, was noteworthy, eye-catching and took the wrecker from being a plain-Jane to the status of a real looker.

The paint and brush had come from a couple builders in "C" Company when Shiell came across a CO_2 fire extinguisher that they could use to quickly cool beer on hot evenings. The fire extinguisher came from a supply guy in Headquarters Company who needed to have a borrowed jeep pulled out of a ditch before his commanding officer came back from a meeting. Shiell obliged, the supply guy supplied, the beer was cooled and the wrecker's wheels perked up, everything in its time.

It did not take a Rembrandt to do the job, just a steady hand and a spinning wheel so the paint would flow on evenly. In a couple hours, Shiell had jacked up, cleaned and painted all six wheels. Then, perhaps as an afterthought, he also did the spare tire mounted on the back of the cab. Facing to the rear, it was a statement to anyone behind that this was one classy rig rolling down the road in front of them.

When not in use, the wrecker spent most of its time in the middle of the yard in front of the mechanics' shop where the painted wheel rims and clean machine drew a fair amount of attention. Some of the attention, unfortunately, was from the Master Chief who apparently was not a lover of art or embellishments, and decidedly unenthusiastic about the effects of silver paint over olive drab—even in minor amounts.

After some days of critiquing the wrecker from his military point of view, the Master Chief called Shiell into his office and wanted to know why he had painted the wheel rims the way he did. Shiell reportedly said, "I think it makes the wrecker look better."

"Better than what?" asked the Master Chief.

"Better than not being painted," said Shiell.

"Oh, the wheel rims weren't painted when it was delivered?"

"Yes, they were painted," said Shiell, "I meant the silver paint made the wheels look better."

"Better than what?" asked the Master Chief again.

"Better than not being painted," said Shiell for the second time.

"Petty Officer Shiell," said the Master Chief, "I think we're stuck here and you're not getting us out of the ditch. I don't think they look better at all. In fact, Shiell, I want you to get some olive drab paint from the storeroom today and repaint the rims in their original issued color. Do you have any questions about that directive?"

"No sir," said Shiell, and the snazzy wrecker quickly reverted to being a plain-Jane that same afternoon. In a few days and the weeks that followed, it became an even plainer-Jane as the mud, dust and dirt caked on. According to Shiell, though, it was just camouflage so nobody could see him coming—or going. In fact, he got lost a lot after that and nobody seemed to notice when the wrecker was not standing out front.

XXII

Eeny, Meeny, Miny...

From Da Nang, the twin-engine AC-47 cruised over the South China Sea for nearly five hours before skirting Corregidor and landing south of Manila. The airplane brought over two dozen men for R&R and would come back to pick them up five days later. The captain and co-pilot took care of everything on the flight, including handling the luggage; and, when everyone had disembarked and the baggage was off-loaded, the two men pointed from the cargo door toward a Quonset hut on the edge of the runway. The rear door was closed a moment later, followed by the front door and engines turned over for the return trip.

Inside the Quonset hut, two rows of red vinyl chairs, back to back, stretched along the centerline of the long, narrow room. The seats were hooked together by chrome arms that were dull in the hazy light filtered through windows long in need of washing. As the soldiers entered, a middle-aged Philippine woman greeted them. "Welcome to the Philippines," she said. "Please have a seat so we can take care of business and get you on your way. Taxies and buses will arrive in a few minutes to take you to your hotel and all you will need to do is tell them where you would like to go. If you do not have a hotel, I have lists here to choose from. Please raise your hand if you would like to have one." She was graceful, attractive and spoke fluent English—the perfect woman for men who had not seen one in months. Cow and R.P. raised their hands along with everyone else.

Nearly three dozen hotels were on the list as Cow scanned the options. "Jesus," he said, "not a Hilton or Holiday Inn anywhere. You want to shed a little light on this?"

Under his breath and nodding his head toward the woman, R.P. said, "She could shed some light on me."

Most of the hotels were identified as being in Manila but a few were in Quezon City, Caloocan, and Pasay. A black soldier with Army insignia asked the woman, "How are we supposed to choose when we don't know anything about 'em?"

Shrugging her shoulders, she said, "I can't recommend one over another, you will have to make that choice. Sorry."

R.P. leaned toward Cow on his right and asked, "What do you think?"

Cow, in mock response, shrugged his shoulders as the woman had just done in front of them. "Sorry," he said, "I can't recommend one over the other."

Another black soldier sat on R.P.'s left. He was studying the same list when Cow added, "But I know how to choose one," and punctuated the beat of his words with his index finger as he went down the line, "ee-ny, mee-ny, mi-ny, mo, catch the nig-ger by the toe."

Almost instantly, the soldier leaned forward past R.P. and said to Cow, "What did you say?"

Cow's reply was equally instant and sheepish as he realized what he had said and mumbled, "I'm sorry, I didn't mean that." Looking into the angry face, he did not know what else to say and repeated, "I am sorry, I didn't mean that." The offended soldier, however, stood up and walked over to a group of his friends who were already waiting for rides. They could have gone out but the hut had air conditioning and it was cooler inside. Cow knew he had made a big mistake and watched the soldier out of the corner of his eye while trying to concentrate on a selection.

"This one sounds about right," he said at last pointing to the Century Park Hotel. "At least it's a name I can recognize and understand."

With his head still down and again in a lowered voice, R.P. said, "And its downtown. You know, you're gonna to get us into a lot of trouble if you don't watch your mouth."

"Yeah, I know. I didn't mean it that way; it's just a rhyme from when I was a kid."

"Maybe," said R.P., "but you're going to have to watch it, that guy's pissed."

Cow looked up from the list to find the soldier and his friends staring at him. There were five Negro soldiers in uniform and they kept their eyes trained on Cow until the woman announced from the doorway that the downtown van had arrived. R.P. got up and walked toward the door with Cow following close behind.

"Maybe I should go over to apologize once more," Cow whispered, but R.P. kept up his pace through the door into the heat outside.

"Let sleeping dogs lie," he said, once the door closed behind them. "You're just lookin' to get us killed in there. Let's get in this van and away from here before we find out who's carrying a weapon."

The downtown vehicle was a burgundy Range Rover with "Century Park" painted in large gold script across the side doors. There was room for seven passengers but only four were going. The driver tossed their luggage onto the roof rack and said, "I take you Century Park. Get in, we go, quick-quick."

R.P. and Cow climbed into the back seat followed by the other two soldiers, one black and one white, who got into the middle. The black soldier turned around to Cow as soon as they were underway and Cow saw he was one of the friends, but not the guy who bore the brunt of his big mouth. The soldier stared at Cow for a moment and then said, "I'm going to forget what you said in there, but you better forget what you said in there too," and he turned back to the front.

Cow started to say again, "I didn't…" but stopped. He could not erase his earlier words. It was a dumb, insulting, infuriating, hurtful thing to have said, but he had never thought about it like that before. It was a leftover, a hangover from being a kid in Wisconsin where you grew up with people who told racist jokes but did not think of themselves as racists. The same kind of place where many drank to excess but insisted that they were not alcoholics because they always got up and went to work on time.

The single black person Cow had ever met before joining the Navy was on an escapade to Green Bay one night when he shook hands with a Packer player who was a big man with huge hands and a local hero. The only other minorities he ever saw were the ones who stopped at the local drive-in on the edge of town where they were served paper cups of root beer so the white patrons would not have to use the same glasses later on.

Some people asked, "Why do they even stop around here?" as if the highway, the drive-in and the town were off limits to anyone who was not white. He knew some people thought it ought to work that way—the way the migrants did it when they came up for summer jobs at the canning factory. You never saw them in town except maybe at the grocery store. Other than that, as far as most anyone knew, they never left the bare-wood shacks behind the pea vine stack.

Cow remembered peering into an empty room one time when he had to go there to load the farm's share of the stinking fermented vines. It was late fall so everyone was gone for the year and he could have walked right in because there was no door to keep him out of the squalid housing. Instead, he looked in through a glassless window at the twisted gray floorboards and the shafts of light, speckled with dust, shining down through open cracks in the roof.

"But thank goodness," he had heard it said, "at least those people know enough not to be comin' to the drive-in when they ride in and out of town under canvas in the back of a truck."

XXIII

Change of Watch

Cow carefully unfolded his pressed greens, just back from the base laundry, and brushed off his jungle boots. His starched hat with the third-class crow sat on his rack. The crow, wings spread above a single chevron, was flat black so it would not glare and attract sniper fire. Next to the hat, his coiled web belt waited with its polished brass buckle. The bright shine had been specifically ordered for the occasion, snipers or not.

After pulling on the starched fatigues, his boots followed and he bloused the pant legs for the first time in months. The web belt was next and he took care not to get finger prints on the brass while adjusting his gig line. An ammo belt with two pouches was last. One pouch had three clips for his M-16 rifle while the other held his camera. Normally, he would have worn three pouches, one for the Camera and two for ammo, but today, detail was as important as his Fujica and one pouch had to be left behind.

Careful not to crease his hat or break down its starched points, Cow rolled the bill slightly in his cupped hands and put it on straight. Squared away was not his usual modus operandi but this was not a usual day.

A deuce and a half stopped in front of the mess hall at exactly 10:00 a.m. to pick up the honor guard. Twenty-one men climbed in and rode on wooden seats under a canvas roof trying to keep the dirt off their clean fatigues and oiled rifles. North of the bridge over the Han River, close to downtown Da Nang, the truck turned off the main highway to follow a short, paved circular drive down to the water's edge. Near the shoreline, a small amphitheater stood ready and spoke of formality in the middle of a war zone. Low concrete walls curved back from the riverbank enclosing a mosaic stone terrace with a lectern in the middle. Three rows of metal folding chairs faced the lectern with room behind for the honor guard. The day was going to be very warm and the shadows from the lectern and chairs shortened as the sun climbed overhead heating the stone floor.

General William Childs Westmoreland came to South Vietnam in 1964 and was about to go home after a few words up and down the country. The honor guard had been standing and waiting for nearly an hour before a black sedan finally arrived. Parked near the end of the concrete walls, the driver got out and opened a rear door for the General. Apparently alone in the car, a second sedan pulled up with the General's support staff and audience as he got out.

Cow lifted the Fujica from his ammo pouch, closed down the aperture and increased the shutter speed because of the bright sunlight. The men were "At Ease" and he began taking pictures of the General and his entourage coming forward. He saw no other guests, but the Fujica caught it all: the General; the staff; the stern face in front and the almost balmy visages behind. In one profile, the four stars on Westmoreland's collar aligned with the lobe of his ear to look like earrings on a gypsy prince. Even faced with it, the General's position and level of authority was nearly incomprehensible to Cow near the bottom of the military food chain.

The viewfinder was still to his eye when a touch on Cow's shoulder made him flinch. Without a word spoken, yet the message intact, he put the camera back into his ammo pouch and pulled down the fitted canvas cover. The officer in charge of the honor guard watched until the pouch was closed before saying, "You know: you should only have ammo in there, just in case. You never know about snipers."

"Yes, Sir," said Cow, grasping his rifle from where it rested against his leg. But Jesus, he thought, we are in the middle of Da Nang with the commanding general, air support all around and you are worried about one ammo pouch? Maybe I should have blackened my belt buckle instead!

Unfazed by Cow's thoughts, the officer tensed as an aide-de-camp stepped to the lectern. In a moment of silence, before the aide spoke, the officer called the honor guard to attention and rifles snapped to shoulders. The men, standing stiffly, heard the short introduction, even if they were not listening, until the General came forward to give his only order of the morning: "Honor Guard—Parade Rest."

Westmoreland directed a half-million American soldiers in Vietnam. His orders, loosely interpreted, were to defeat the Viet Cong and stop the spread of communism in Southeast Asia. Using the microphone before him, he expanded on that theme by saying a difference was being made and the war was being won. Tet was a victory for us, he insisted, not the Viet Cong, and the American people supported efforts to win over the hearts and minds of the Vietnamese.

The General concluded by saying he was proud to have served on behalf of President Lyndon Baines Johnson and would work with renewed diligence to make Vietnam a free democratic society when he joined the Joint Chiefs of Staff. Finished, he saluted, pivoted and strode briskly back to the car where his driver had already opened the door for him.

The small assemblage, far less than the number needed for three rows of chairs, followed the General away. A minute later, the officer in charge bellowed, "Honor Guard: Dismissed!" and turned away himself. In a brisk walk back to his jeep, the officer passed the deuce and a half and motioned for the driver to come forward to pick up the men dawdling along behind him. Cow, with his camera out again, saw the truck advancing and took a picture of the black exhaust rising from the diesel's stack. In the calm and heat of midday, the sooty remnants of incomplete combustion rose like an exclamation point at the end of the General's résumé.

XXIV

Multiculturalism

There was plenty of hot water after the first rush of reveille and Cow stood alone in the shower. He had stayed in bed with his pillow over his head trying to keep the light and noise out because there was no need to get up until he had to—at least fifteen minutes after everyone else had left. It was his week to pick up the trash and sweep out the hut, but he also knew how to turn the ten-minute task into an hour or more of free time with no one looking over his shoulder.

Late in the early morning, the sun was already above the horizon as Cow began his shower and rubbed soap into his short dark hair. He always started on top and worked his way down. The hot drops of water pelted his neck and stung his back until he turned around to let the steamy flood rinse him clean. The shower room had no closing doors, partitions or curtains, so from where he stood under the spray he could see out through the entryway. His clothes and shaving kit waited on a bench to the right of the opening and, beyond the bench, a row of sinks lined the end wall with mirrors and lights above. A few of the bulbs still burned, though collectively adding little to the rectangle of sunlight coming through the entrance. With the luxury of plenty of hot water raining down, he watched the geometric lines of sun and shadow move slowly across the concrete floor. It was an extravagance only to be had occasionally when everyone else had already departed.

This was shaping up to be a very good day and Cow was even later than usual with plenty of excuses if asked. Forearmed, he was soaking up the solitude until he looked out to see four young Vietnamese women approaching with cleaning pails. They walked four abreast in sandals, each with the traditional pointed straw hat, shinny black pants, and a flowing tunic on top. The tunics, two white, one blue, and the last in lavender, were split on both sides from hip to ankle and flared with each step. As the girls came forward, he watched, naked under the rushing water, wondering what they wore beneath. He also thought they could wait until he was done and then turned slowly in a circle under the hot spray, eyes closed and face turned upward. He was in no hurry and still had to shave and dress.

When he opened his eyes, however, the girls, or women, he was not sure which, were silhouetted in the entryway, dark against the light. Beyond the sound of the running water, he could hear them talking even if he could not understand their words or actually see their faces in the glow that surrounded them. No one moved. He remained under the shower as if it was a curtain around him and they stood there blocking much of the sun, everyone probably thinking that it was now too dim to see clearly what they were clearly seeing. Still, Cow did not attempt get his towel or clothing. They can wait, he thought again, staying under the running water.

But they did not wait, and a moment later, the four females filed into the shower room. They seemed to pay no attention to Cow and he was unsure if they even noticed that he was standing there with his mouth open and his wondering imagination at half-staff. Turning on the remaining lights above the mirrors, they bent to their tasks. The pails with their cleaning supplies sat on the floor and a straw hat hung in the middle of each back as they washed and wiped the sinks. In four of the mirrors, long black hair framed oval faces and bright eyes that glanced back at the running shower from time to time. And Cow was not sure if they were smiling or laughing.

XXV

Paper Princess

Crayons could match the imagination when reality could not. Colored pencils too. Chalk, ink and, in an emergency, even a bullet's lead tip would do. The idea was complex, eternal, simple and primitive. When one-hundred days felt like an eternity and could easily be more than a lifetime, square one on a short-timers calendar commenced the countdown.

Nearly everybody had one somewhere: inside backpacks or ammo pouches, tacked to a crate or tree, taped to the insides of hatch covers or the back of the door-gunner's seat. They were always handy and celebrated in simple artistic fashion. One hundred blocks made the whole and the countdown usually started at the fingertips or toes. The idea was to work backward until you were "In like Flynn!" Colored in, checked off or counted down, each block was another day on the way out of Vietnam.

Nobody seemed to know where they came from but they were available almost everywhere. In reality, some yeoman or clerk with access to a duplicating machine probably decided to have some fun and make a little money on the side. At a quarter each, multiplied by six hundred thousand soldiers year in and year out, the potential annual income was a hundred and fifty grand—not bad for a crude drawing of a naked woman.

Somewhere between art and fantasy, Cow was taking the low road when he crossed off each day with a nondescript "X". He was not sure when he was leaving, but everything was moving in the right direction. At worst, he was under a hundred days. His enlistment began in March of 1966 under the "Delayed Entry Program" and he began active duty a week after graduating from Hillton High. He and a classmate, Pazzi, enlisted in the Navy with an understanding that they would go through basic training together in something called the "Buddy Program." Under 18 when they joined, both were on a "kiddie cruise" for three years with guaranteed release from active duty the day before their 21st birthdays. After basic, Pazzi was assigned to the U.S.S. Forrestal off Vietnam while Cow joined the Seabees heading for the same place.

Pazzi was set to get out on June 12th, Cow on the 2nd of July. A plan was moving forward, however, and Cow was already waiting for confirmation that he could strike a month off his short-timer's calendar. What he envisioned was being home by Memorial Day with a beer in hand when Pazzi finally showed up thinking he was first.

Unknown to his buddies, Cow had applied for entrance to college and had been accepted starting with the summer session of 1969. With the acceptance in hand, he applied for an "early out" working backward from his birthday. The summer session started the second week of June and he added an extra week to get home and find his way to campus. As such, a hundred days from his birthday, he began his short-timer's calendar on March 25th and applied for a thirty-day early release from active duty.

Thirty-two days later, Cow's X's had begun moving inward toward knees and nipples. He used a black, permanent felt tip marker appropriated from Security's Central Command bunker to cross off each block, but time was getting short if he was going to make the summer session. He was getting anxious, but that is how he stood on April 25th when he finally got word that his request had been approved for a thirty-day early out plus eight days for travel and processing. Counting down to freedom, it left only 30 days and a wakeup in country.

Cow already had six beers and kept looking at the folded papers handed to him that afternoon. He was going home in thirty days and celebrating.

"How short are ya?" someone asked in the EM Club.

"I'm short," said Cow. "So short I could free fall off this here beer can. So short that the edges of these papers are starting to look like the walls of the Grand Canyon. So short that I can barely see any of you guys from down here without binoculars. And I'm a hell of a lot shorter than you!"

When R.P. sat down, Cow began again. "Look at this shit, thirty days and a wake-up, and I'm out o' this hole!" He stood up and took long quick steps to the bar where he threw down a wrinkled dollar of military script. Coming back, he brought six more beers and his ten-cent note.

R.P. grabbed a cold one and popped the top. "Here's to ya," he said, "and all us poor bastards who'll watch ya ride out the gate." He tipped up the can and emptied it in one try. It had been another scorcher as the sun climbed higher trying to leave the rainy season behind. The 12 ounces of beer slid down R.P.'s throat so quickly it barely stopped his lament. "God, I wish I was out of this fucking place," he said, while setting his empty on the table and picking up another full can.

Willy put his beer down too and lit a cigarette. "Look at it this way," he said, "us being over here gives all those pukes back home a shot at the women. Otherwise they'd all be bachelors forever. Just think what you're doin' for your fellow man. You don't want all those girls chasin' ya down the street for a bite 'a' your ass. You need a little freedom an' this is it. What ya think, Benny?"

"I think if there was a girl around here I'd chase her down the street till I caught her. I keep looking for one at the bottom of these here beer cans but just can't find any."

"Now there's an idea," said Willy. "Girl in a can— pop a top and out jumps Jeannie. Ya wanna sniff the top to see if she's still in here?" He threw his empty can across the table at Benny who twisted his shoulder out of the way and let it fly by. It fell on the floor behind him and someone at the next table flattened it with his boot heel before kicking it back.

Willy jumped up in mock agitation yelling at the kicker, "Now look what ya done, my girlfriend was in there, and now, thanks to you, she's all cramped up!" Three empty beer cans sailed at Willy's head as he ducked back down into his chair laughing.

Cow checked the dates on the paper again and looked up at his friends horsing around. He guessed he would miss them, some of them anyway, maybe all of them. Looking into the top of his beer can, he understood that he would be the only one leaving. They were stuck and that was sobering, even after seven or eight beers.

R.P. was talking about work in the tire shop and Willy crushed another empty can half listening. Benny drummed his fingers on the table and began waving to someone coming through the door. Cow could hear the buzz around the room but was not listening, just looking until his eyes and ears closed and left everyone behind. For a moment, he was alone with only thirty days to go. Thirty days. No more shit beer with formaldehyde, no more mud or burning sun, no more stinking latrines or mortars at midnight. Thirty days and they could take this place and shove it.

"Here's to beating Pazzi home," he said, lifting his PBR with clearing eyes and ears. Later that night he crossed thirty-nine days off his paper princess ending just below her belly button. Thirty-nine in case he did not remember in the morning.

XXVI

Slots

The clerk stopped halfway down the office stair and yelled out over the bays below, "Anybody want to go to Hawaii?"

Cow, near the bottom of the stairway for no particular reason and just the luck of it, instantly shouted back, "Yeah, when do I leave?"

"Can you be ready in two hours?"

"Hell," Cow said, "I can be ready in twenty minutes."

"Use 'em or loose 'em," said the clerk. "Come on up and I'll type out the orders. Will need to call over to the dispensary for copies of your shot records too."

Cow took the steps two at a time with his hat already in hand before he entered. The clerk's desk was first in a row of three, followed by the Master Chief and Company Commander. Each appeared to have a cushioned chair and the clerk dropped softly into his. Rolling paper into his typewriter, he adjusted the tabs while glancing at Cow's fatigues for the spelling of his name.

Cow's name, however, was not on his fatigues, only his initials, and he began to spell out Barthochowski as he always did. "B as in Bravo, A as in Alpha, R as in Romeo, T as in Tango, H as in Hotel, O as in Oscar, C as in Charlie, H as in Hotel, O as in Oscar, W as in Whiskey, S-K-I as in Ski." It was an adapted military ritual he had adopted early on.

The rendition caused the Master Chief to look up and adjust his glasses. The glasses were nearly at the end of his nose and he used both hands to bring them back to the bridge. "How come that isn't on your uniform, Barthochowski? Is that regulation?"

"Yes, sir!" said Cow. "In boot camp the name was too long for the stencil so they used my initials. It's been the same ever since."

"Hmmmm," groaned the Master Chief as he tipped his face back to his work and the glasses immediately began their downhill slide.

The typewriter stopped clicking and the platen whined as the clerk pulled out the page. He stapled a cover sheet to the general orders and handed them to Cow. "Take these to the disburser who'll provide you with currency. Then stop at the dispensary for a copy of your shot records to take with you and be back here in ninety minutes."

"You bet," said Cow, retreating carefully through the door before bounding down the steps. Hawaii meant nearly two weeks away from Quang Tri with less than a month left in Vietnam. He could hardly believe his luck.

It was still misting outside as it had been for the past four weeks or more. Light mist, heavy mist, rainy mist and down-pouring mist. Cow would not miss any of it and kept to the plank walkways as much as he could, surfing on the mud

164

below whenever the boards shifted beneath his feet. Seven days in Hawaii, two days flying, a day down to Da Nang and a day back could easily eat up a dozen days out of his last twenty-five. If he took advantage of opportunities, he might be able to stretch it into two full weeks. "Son-of-a-bitch!" he said to himself breaking into a skidding run on the sloppy path to the disburser's office. He wanted to get going before anybody figured out how short he really was.

One Seabee stood in front of the barred window when Cow came in letting the door slam behind. The sharp crack, like an unexpected shot, caused the poor guy nearly to fumble the money he was returning. His nerves were not doing well and although he managed to hang on to the cash, lost track of the amount and had to start over counting.

Cow overheard the disburser say through his window, "Sure is a shame not to be going."

"Yeah, but there's nothing I can do about it," came the reply as a stack of twenties was pushed under the metal bars in the window. "Should be eight hundred."

Cow knew the story. Everyone knew the story by breakfast: another love story re-written from the hometown perspective. It was nothing new—he was here, she was there. He would get over it, but not soon enough to go to Hawaii alone.

The door now slammed behind Cow as he pushed his papers beneath the bars. "I think I'll only need four hundred—whoever said two can live as cheap as one?"

"You better take five," said the disburser, "just to be on the safe side. You get his slot?"

"Use it or loose it," said Cow, "I guess I was in the right spot at the right time. Maybe they'll have some sunshine in Honolulu. Sure will be nice to get out of this mud!"

"...sixty, eighty, one hundred; makes five hundred U.S. dollars. Now, remember, this is not to be spent anywhere in country or you can be arrested for passing currency. Got that?" Cow nodded in the affirmative and the disburser slid a receipt under the bars. "Print your name on the first line, sign on the second," he said.

Finished signing for the money, Cow passed the receipt back and picked up the stack of bills. "Thanks a lot," he said turning toward the door just as it was being pulled open by the clerk carrying a handful of papers.

"Excuse me," said the clerk, brushing and bumping past to get to the window. Cow grabbed for the door before it slammed again and eased himself out. He guided the door with one hand while nonchalantly turning the passage lock with the other. Gently closed with a soft click, he was ten steps away when he heard the clerk slam into the locked door. "Jesus, what the hell?" could be heard halfway to the dispensary.

"That's using your head," crowed the disburser. "Would you please make sure it's unlocked when you go out? Happens sometimes."

The clerk caught up to Cow by the time he climbed the wooden steps to the dispensary. Cow was first through the door but the clerk went around him to the corpsman's desk. "I called you about a copy of Barthochowski's records for the office. He has to leave in an hour. Are they ready?"

"Oh, they're probably here," said the corpsman looking at the initials on Cow's greens. "How do you spell that?" he asked, and Cow began the routine again: "B as in Bravo, A as in Alpha, R as in Romeo...."

The corpsman nonchalantly jotted down the letters and went to retrieve the records while Cow and the clerk waited. Standing there, Cow's grease stained shirt and muddied pants were no match for the clerk's clean greens. It was as if they were from two different worlds: one of grease and grime, the other of polished boots and brass, starch and creases.

"I suppose it's nice working up there in the air conditioning and all," said Cow, but the clerk ignored him and Cow continued unacknowledged. "We could always use a little of that cool air out in the shop but that's never gonna happen, I suppose."

Standing in front of the corpsman's desk, the clerk's arms were folded across his chest until he let them down to finger tap his impatience on the desktop.

"It must be interesting to know about everything that goes on in the company," said Cow, trying again to make small talk.

The clerk, however, was not cooperating. "Barthochowski," he said, "you do your job and I'll do mine. I know it's hard to understand, but being in the front seat of that office is no picnic either. I know you're out of here in a few weeks and somebody else should be taking this slot, but I just need to get this done and back to work. Maybe someday you and a few of your friends will be able to appreciate that."

The corpsman came back and handed two sheets of paper to each of them. "Thank you," said Cow, before turning to the clerk. "Is there anything else that I need?" he asked. But the clerk did not hear him, or at least did not answer, because he had turned too and gave the door a good shove as he went out.

Springs recoiling, the door swung back and slammed shut. The corpsman raised his eyebrows in reaction while slowly shaking his head. "Some day," he said, pursing his lips, "some day." He was leaning forward on his arms with two hands flat on the desk in front of him. His greens were faded and slightly frayed along seams rubbed white from washing. "No," he added, as if he had been asked the question, "you're up to date and good to go. Watch your step on the way out."

XXVII

The Blue Goose

The goose was both ubiquitous and a contradiction. A martini rode in her wing fingers and she looked as if she were about to strut right off the back of the blue T-shirts she graced. A white goose, she seemed to be in a hurry, though obviously going nowhere, following the white bubbles floating above her white glass. Her bill was open as if she were catching a breath, snapping at the bubbles or having a last word in a short conversation. Follow me, she might have said, down the path of white block letters that spelled out "The Blue Goose—Honolulu" beneath her feet. Like a line that invited crossing, she extended an invitation to move inland away from the sand and surf of Waikiki.

Cow had rolled under the cuffs of his long sleeves because it had been a warm walk from his one-room, one-week efficiency on Prince Edward Street. Midmorning, he had found his way to Ala Wai Boulevard where it bordered a canal with a busy golf course on the other side. His side, though, was completely deserted except for one tall blond jogger who had come toward him on the wide sidewalk. She wore white short shorts and a thin white blouse with breasts bouncing freely beneath. He tried not to stare but could not pull his eyes away from her long bronze legs, shifting chest and knowing smile. After she passed, he turned and watched her from behind as she ran away.

The boulevard paralleled the canal for more than a mile before a bridge crossed at McCully Street. A block later, he took a right on Kapiolani until he stumbled, almost literally, onto University Avenue. His intention was to find the University of Hawaii campus, although, where King Street crossed, an "Open" sign hanging on the corner door of The Blue Goose lured him in. The bar was an unexpected find and he was thirsty from the long walk even if it was still well before noon.

The bartender, small and wiry with shoulder length hair, quickly opened a bottle of San Miguel, rang up the sale and went back to his busywork. White geese on blue t-shirts were everywhere in the bar, pinned to the walls and hung from the ceiling. Twelve tables, painted on top like children's alphabet blocks, were in disarray and a waitress worked to rearrange them until the letters spelled out the bar's name as intended.

Cow watched her move the tables because, like the jogger with the long legs, she was much of what was missing in Vietnam. When he came in, the long legs had shifted back to the white goose chasing martinis from T-shirt to T-shirt. In a few moments, however, they became attached to the waitress as she bent over in her mini-skirt shoving the tables around the room.

There were no other patrons in the bar and Cow would have liked to talk to her but did not know how to start the conversation. He was at odds with the world around him and knew it. Even in jeans and a paisley shirt, he did not fit in because a quick glance at his heavy black shoes and military haircut told anyone that he was a soldier and not some kid from college.

The difference was elementary, beginning with the long hair of the bartender and ending somewhere near the hemline of the waitress's short skirt. In the year and a half that he had been in Vietnam, hemlines had risen from knee to upper thigh as resistance to the war had gone up. He was visiting a world in transition, almost inside out, where girls lay on Waikiki Beach in their white underwear, joggers went braless in thin white blouses, white panties flashed under short skirts and the white goose toasted it all.

"Another?" the bartender asked and Cow broke his daydream by mouthing no and shaking his head. Two quarters lay on the bar and he pushed them forward as he spun around on the stool to leave. Coming around, he nearly bumped into a young man standing directly behind him—someone he had not seen or heard come in. The guy stepped back slightly, but still faced Cow with a glass of beer in one hand and a cigarette in the other.

"Need help?" he asked.

"Need what?"

"Do you need help? You don't have to go back, ya know."

"Back where?" asked Cow, still somewhat in the dark.

"There are people here who can help you if you don't want to go back."

In the vague conversation, an alternative was opening. "I appreciate the offer," said Cow, "but I only have two weeks left when I get back."

"That can be two long weeks and I've been there. If you change your mind, come back and ask for Dan. The bartender knows how to get in touch. We have friends in Canada and South America who can help."

Cow said, "Thanks, but it's only for two more weeks and I think I can handle it."

"The offer's always open," said Dan, taking a sip of his beer, a drag on the cigarette and turning toward the waitress who now stood watching at the end of the bar.

Walking out, Cow could feel all of their eyes on his back until the door closed behind him. Again, the sun was bright outside and he quickly felt its heat through his shirt. Realizing he had forgotten to ask how to get to the University, he wandered some of the nearby streets thinking about never having thought about not going back. It was an odd sensation, an unanticipated option that left him ill at ease. He was not naïve, but at this point the possibility, the reality, of bailing out was disconcerting and dark.

Later, the university search abandoned, Cow retraced his steps past The Blue Goose and was already back on Kapiolani before thinking that he should have bought one of the T-shirts.

XXVIII

Bonus

The Personnel Officer's job was to give the reenlistment speech—Cow's job was to ignore it. Summoned three times, he had crumpled the paper request each time before throwing it away. He was not going to re-up and there was no use in talking about it. No use, that was, until the Master Chief's hand came down on his shoulder. "Report to the Personnel Office," he said, "and don't get lost between here and there. They are waiting for you NOW!"

With unequivocal direction and only ten days left in country, Cow stepped off the concrete shop floor and began trudging through the mud of the late rainy season. He stomped hard in the sloppiest places to splash his boots and pant legs, intending to leave a trail on the floor and chairs when he got there. It was childish, he knew; but so what, he thought, everything else was inside out too. Sometimes he was in a theater of war, at other times the war played out as if the whole thing was from the theater of the absurd. It only depended upon the day, the time and circumstances.

The muddy tracks were impressive coming through the door and across the plywood floor. Cow held his cap in his left hand as a clerk motioned him forward into a second room where a Lieutenant Commander sat at his desk writing.

Entering, Cow gave a full salute and said, "Barthochowski, reporting as ordered, SIR!"

"At ease, and sit down," said the officer without looking up—or down at the mud trailing into his office. "This is just a formality for many of you and it won't take long. Have you ever thought of extending your enlistment in the Navy?"

"No," said Cow, in a clipped response with the chips still resting heavily on his shoulders.

"There is a sizable reenlistment bonus available if you should choose to do so. I can authorize up to eighteen hundred dollars for each year you extend. That would mean a check in excess of ten thousand dollars if you were to reenlist for six more years. A sizable sum, as I have said."

"No, thank you," said Cow, "unless you can guarantee exactly where I would go and for how long. I would like to spend a winter in Antarctica just for the hell of it." Cow knew the Personnel Officer could not guarantee anything. Besides, if the officer had looked at his records, he already knew of the approved early out for college.

"I'm sorry," said the Lieutenant Commander as he looked up and his eyes caught sight of the muddy trail, "but I'm not in a position to guarantee assignments. Is there anything else that might make you reconsider?"

"No. I just want to get out of here in one piece and never come back."

"Very well," he said. "I'll indicate here that you have declined our reenlistment offer. And if you will sign this form where I have checked 'None' we'll consider the interview complete."

Cow gave the Reenlistment Opportunities paper -a cursory glance and quickly followed all of the starred options down to the checked box. His typed name appeared below the signature line and he stood to sign the paper on the desk with a final scrawled flourish.

The officer offered his hand across the desk and said, "Thank you for coming in. Looks like it's still raining outside."

"Yes, Sir," said Cow, "I believe it is," and lightly shook the extended hand before coming to full attention and saluting again.

This time, the Lieutenant Commander raised his right hand to his forehead and let his elbow slide down his side in a half-hearted salute that said much more than his final word, "Dismissed."

As Cow did an about-face, he caught sight of the chair where he had sat and the mud he had brought in. For a moment, he felt sorry for making the mess but that quickly evaporated as he walked out feeling freer than he had been for over three years. There would be no hash marks on his sleeve.

Returning to the shop, Cow came face-to-face with the youngest old-timer he knew and stepped off the planks to let him pass. Ray was not wearing a hash mark yet, but he would be, soon enough, and it might begin to cover that tattoo he was always trying to rub off his left forearm. It was hard for Ray to leave the tattoo alone. Back in the states, he had shown it off with his new girlfriend's name just a couple days after he had met her. It said 'Jill' with a small red rose above the 'i' and green vines curling around the letters.

Ray had fallen in love at a local bar, just outside the gate, two blocks from base. Usually quiet, he was the shy kind of guy who needed a little prodding to loosen up. As it went, a few drinks released his inhibitions, and, when his affection seemed to be returned in kind, it grabbed him like nothing else ever did. He did not ask many questions and did not want to answer many either. He was in love and trusted that she was in love with him. Life was wonderful and they were going to smell the roses together—forever.

Three weeks later, they were married by a justice of the peace, celebrated with a few beers in the same old place and left for two quick nights in New Orleans. When they came back from the brief honeymoon, the bride went back to her room at a boarding house on the edge of town and Ray came back to the barracks until they could find an apartment. "Her landlady don't want no men in her house and she's one mean some-bitch!" he said.

Because of the ceremony and honeymoon, Ray was already getting short of money before they went looking for an apartment. By midweek, when the cost of reality began to settle in, his new wife encouraged him to stop at the personnel office to consider his options. The good news was almost more than he could have hoped for. If he signed up for six more years on top of what he still had left, the Navy would pay him a bonus of one hundred fifty dollars per month up front—ten thousand, eight hundred dollars.

With nearly four years in already, Ray said he would talk it over with his wife because it meant six more years in the Navy and that would put him on track to become a lifer. The talk must have been short and sweet because by the next afternoon when he came back to the office he was ready to sign. Right after that, the newlyweds went looking for a place of their own and found one. "It's nice and we can afford it now," he told anybody who would listen. "And she'll be safe waiting for me while I'm gone." He was the protector.

The bonus check, cut a day later, was promptly placed in a new joint savings account. Ray was on top of the world: they had ten thousand dollars in the bank with another eight hundred for rent, security deposit, a little furniture and a big bed. The next Sunday afternoon he was still grinning when he got on the bus for a week and a half of training at Camp Shelby, sixty miles north. "Let's hurry up and get 'er done," he said, "so I can get back home. The missus is waiting!" Everyone laughed with him while kicking back in their seats for the lackluster ride out to the chigger-infested piney woods they would call home for the next ten days.

Ray sounded like the most domesticated man in Mississippi. He talked about his wife most of the time unless he had his mess kit in front of him with his mouth full. Sometimes he still talked about her then. He was happier than he had ever been, not even complaining about what was on the menu except for an ad lib about what he supposed should have been there and what his little lady would be cooking when he got home. Mainly, he was just riding it out, wishing and waiting to get back.

The ten days in the yellow pine of southern Mississippi were spent practicing survival skills, work simulations and physical fitness routines. It was also a time to begin knowing what it would feel like to be cut off from family and friends. No newspapers, televisions or telephones were available presenting a prelude of what was to come.

Mail call started on the third day when one or two letters trickled in. Ray, however, did not get any even though he sent one every morning on his way to breakfast. After two more days, he said, "She must have the address wrong," and sent it to her again. After a week, though, he only sent a short note saying he would be home on Wednesday afternoon and they could pick up where they had left off.

Ray missed muster the morning after he got back. About midday, he stopped at the chaplain's office before reporting to the company commander who gave him the rest of the day off to get his affairs in order. Later, he said, "I didn't even notice that the curtains were gone until I opened the front door and stood there with my mouth open. 'Jill,' I called, and her name bounced off those empty walls until it finally hit me square in the forehead. There wasn't a thing in the apartment except my clothes on the floor and my letters in the mailbox."

"I talked to the neighbors but they all said they didn't know anything about it because people are always moving in and out. Then I went over to the bar to check with her friends and they said they hadn't seen her in almost two weeks either. So I had a couple drinks—well, maybe more than a couple—and went back to the apartment where I fell asleep on the floor with my clothes for a pillow.

"When I woke up, the sun was way up. I'd already missed muster so I walked down to the restaurant on the corner for something to eat. After that, I went to the bank just to hear what I already knew. The savings account still has the minimum five dollars in it because she couldn't close it without me and I can't close it without her. Ain't that something? They gave her nine thousand, nine hundred, and ninety five dollars bright an' early on Monday morning about the time we were crawlin' through the swamp at Shelby."

Whenever he spoke, Ray rubbed his fingers over his tattoo as if he were trying to erase it, to remove her memory and make room for the hash marks coming his way.

XXIX

Moo-Who?

Cow was short and sitting tall on top of the water tank he was supposed to be repairing. Not a lot of welding remained, but enough to carry him through and the Senior Chief had not set a deadline. Assigned the hot and onerous task, Cow was determined to milk it to the end—at least to the end of his time in Vietnam if not the conclusion of the project.

What the Senior Chief wanted was a new bottom on his water tank: a quarter inch of plate steel that would stop the leaks, stem the cracks and keep the whole thing from falling off a truck while settling the dust around Quang Tri. What Cow wanted was to get the hell out of Vietnam and working on the water tank was as good as anything until the "Bird of Paradise" could take him home.

Mornings began with muster and coffee while it was still dark. When there was enough light to see the task in front of him, Cow checked the oil in the motor that ran the welder, topped off the fuel tank and strung out the welding cables. After that, a short break for a second cup of coffee was in order while deciding how and when to proceed. How was usually a foregone conclusion, when was much more debatable.

The rainy season was ending and alternating with hot sunny days. On rainy days, Cow did not weld on the tank with amperage flowing everywhere. On sunny days, when the temperature rose almost as fast as the sun, the heat quickly drove him away because the steel got so hot no one could touch it. As a result, with a little procrastinating in the early morning, his window of productive opportunity kept closing and extending the job—likely well past his departure.

Quarter-inch plate steel does not bend easily and the bottom of the tank required sixteen, twelve by forty-eight inch strips to be curved around it. A temporary lever was welded to the end of each plate and a hefty pipe clamp, along with a big hammer, pulled the strips down. The hammer was Cow's favorite tool because each time he struck the steel, the noise reverberating from inside the tank sounded as if a cathedral bell hung over the camp. Sometimes he pounded on the steel just for the fun of it, especially if he was feeling good and short, or it was a very hot day and his mood was moving him. When he was feeling really good, he would bang away in what he said was a reality check designed to add a little excitement to the lifters' humdrum perspective where noise equaled industry.

Between the rain and hot sun, there was plenty of time when no welding was done on the water tank. As a result, the project only inched forward, or around, and left ample opportunity for Cow to work on his self-proclaimed artistry in residence program. It was a one-man undertaking but catching on as finished pieces accumulated around the camp. Particularly in the Alpha Company shop, the EM Club and latrines, randomly designed, torch cut, brass covered steel signs proclaimed "SHORT" in various versions and configurations.

Working under the roof of the welding shop when it was raining or if he was in the need of shade, Cow made the overlapping letters in a loose semi-cursive design with the connecting points maintaining the structural integrity of each piece. Whenever one was completed, he would draw another on more of the quarter inch plate he was supposed to be using for the tank, and start again. His soapstone lines guided the acetylene torch after which he used brazing rod and flux to cover the steel. A grinding wheel took off the high spots and a heavy wire-wheel grinder gave the brass a combed luster.

The work was going well and Cow spent many hours covering torch-cut letters in brass, wire brushing and polishing. No one ever bothered him or asked what he was doing because no one wanted to get near that damn hot tank. Besides, he was usually welding for a little while in the morning, picking up in the afternoon, and there was all that banging, clanging, bell-like hammering during the day. Where there was noise, things had to be happening.

Cow made so many pieces that he used up the battalion's entire supply of brazing rod and had to trade for more with a neighboring outfit. An extra bottle of oxygen and another of acetylene took care of that and he was back in business. Two to three inches high and ten to twenty inches long, each sign reinforced the same critical message:

SHORT

SHORTTIMER

COWISSHORT

SHORTERTHANYOU

TOOSHORT

SOSHORT

SHORTER

SHORTEST

SHORTCAKE

NOSHORTLIFERS

10TOSPEND

5ANDALIVE

COWWASSHORT

COWISGONE

MOO-WHO?

In the rear of the shop, a small chalkboard lent itself to the program. The board was seldom used for anything except occasional cryptic notes or seven letter expletives until Cow began keeping track of how many days he had left. The SHORTERTHANYOU sign sat on top of the chalkboard's frame and set the tone as his number of days declined. Over the course of his last week, others began to join in and the timelines began to take on a life of their own with anticipation, speculation and, perhaps, regret. It all depended upon point of view. Most notably, the Senior Chief must have done his homework and jotted down three thousand, six hundred and thirty two days to go. When Cow first saw the number, he was not sure if he should laugh or cry. Perhaps the Senior Chief was telling him that someone would still be around to finish the tank when Cow broke out of the barn. Either that, or the Senior Chief, with ten years left in his military career, was kicking back at Cow for a change. Either way, down to one day and a wake-up, his piece-de-resistance was finished. A Pegasian bovine with wings and whipping tail was ready for welding to the water tank late the next afternoon.

XXX

Salute

With his seabag thrown onto the bed of the one-ton truck, Cow climbed up after it. Sitting down on the bag, he checked his Timex. It was almost 10:00 a.m. and he was more than ready to get going. As far as he could see, no one was watching or had come out to give him a sendoff. Only the shit burners worked in the distance lighting another pot mixed with diesel fuel and gasoline. For a moment, he watched the black smoke billow out of the cut-off barrels as the frying flames licked over the edge. He could almost smell it and was thankful for being a little upwind on a nearly calm day. Cow's stomach was a little queasy and his head still hurt from all the beer he drank the night before when they toasted his leaving and celebrated all their good luck so far. His eyes, behind sunglasses, were bloodshot and bleary, but it made no difference now. Orders in pocket and flying bovine welded to the water tank, he was heading home.

Sitting on his seabag, hunched over with hands on his knees, Cow was taking it easy because this was no time to do anything stupid. Stories were abundant of guys who burned their seabags outside main gates as a final gesture of their heart-felt feelings only to be hauled back in. Likewise, tales traveled the scuttlebutt circuit about final swings at some bastard and not getting to go. Cow had heard it all and was not going to let them get to him that way.

The sun beat down on his newest, dark-green fatigues and he was already getting hot by the time the driver came out of the personnel office walking toward the truck. "All set?" the operator asked from below and climbed into the cab before getting an answer. Cow was more than set when the twisting growl of the starter brought the truck to life. Bracing, he heard the transmission click into gear and felt the vibration of the clutch engaging. They did not have far to go, the camp gate was only a couple hundred yards, the landing zone just a mile down the road and from there he would catch a chopper to Da Nang.

Picking up speed, the truck kicked up two windrows of dust to cover the road behind them. Cow straightened slightly overcoming inertia to take one last look at a place he never wanted to see again. It was a study in a single, solitary earth tone where everything was the same cocoa colored brown. Ground, roofs, faded sandbags and muddied machinery all blended into each other until almost nothing was identifiable or distinct.

Bracing again, the truck stopped at the main gate while the trailing dust, as though adding insult to injury, rolled up and over the truck from behind. In the dirty air, a clipboard was passed up for a final signing. Handed back, Cow looked to his left at the "A" Company yard where R.P. was now walking out toward the tire truck. Already feeling disconnected, Cow watched and wondered if he would ever see his pal again. Probably not, he thought, taking in the whole sweep of the tan camp as the truck began moving once more.

If it was not dust and dirt they had lived in, it was mud and crud. It was in his eyes and ears, mouth and throat, body and soul. Facing backward, he rode out with the color drained from his imagination, elbows tucked in tight, and fingers clamped to his knees. Almost involuntarily then, as the truck was shifted into second gear and the guard turned to re-hang his clipboard, Cow raised both arms with two single-fingered salutes held high. Words could say no more for the time and place.

Turning onto the dirt highway, the driver shifted into third and Cow brought his arms down quickly to balance and swing around. Facing forward, the hot air rushed past feeling a little cooler and he sucked it in before spitting out grit from the earlier backwash. Looking forward, almost everything was behind him where the days would go on as if he had never been there and was never coming back.

XXXI

Five Nights

From Quang Tri, a helicopter hop on a Jolly Green Giant brought Cow to Da Nang to wait for a flight out. Unassigned, he spent the first two days at the China Beach USO, the new PX at Freedom Hill and a couple EM clubs that opened early. The nights, however, had him sweating and it was unnerving to think that some mortar round had his name on it. He knew he was not the target, that was the deep-water supply port near the temporary barracks, but he also knew that mortars did not know the difference.

The first night he went to sleep rather naively in relative security until pulled from his slumber by the detonating "thump, thump, thump" of incoming rounds. He instinctively rolled off his rack onto the floor, grabbing his helmet and flak jacket as he dropped. Rolling beneath the spring and mattress, he was already fully awake by the time a nearby siren went off. In the siren's circuitous trip, the screaming alarm rose and fell in repeated crescendos while the thumps and thuds kept his hands shaking, clammy cold. The holding area was well fortified, but not against flying grenades and he stayed under the bunk when the siren faded. He had been through it many times but not so close to the finish line.

The second night repeated the first only starting earlier and lasting longer. Once again, Cow was under his bed with his flak jacket strapped tight and helmet pulled down low. The frequency of the mortar rounds increased until they seemed to have an almost musical cadence: "thum-thump," "thum-thump," "thum-thump, thum-thump, thum-thump." The rounds were so near that sometimes Cow thought he could hear the flying whine of the projectiles. But maybe not, he also considered, because he was inside, under his rack with his helmet on, which made everything hard to hear— especially through all the noise. Of course, if it was all in his head, the voice of experience, so to speak, there was no way to stop or corral it. In the morning, as if commenting on this consideration, his head ached from the blowup.

The real target was the ammunition being unloaded nearby. With only six piers, many ships anchored out in the harbor with barges shuttling their explosive cargoes to shore. The lights needed to work at night set the stage and the barges became the proverbial ducks on a pond. The ideal target was a loaded barge tied next to a loaded ship alongside another loaded ship, all not far from the temporary barracks.

Once on shore, the bombs and bullets were trucked to the new ammunition supply point and Cow remembered when the previous ASP blew up on his first tour. On that afternoon he had watched dark clouds roll overhead in huge waves like an angry gray, upside down sea while the exploding bombs shook the ground where he stood from five miles away. The explosions went on all day and into the night like a summer storm with distant thunder and lighting. Afterward, the conflagration fueled speculation that the North Vietnamese might attack while ammunition supplies were low and the vulnerability churned stomachs keeping many men near sleepless for days on end.

Cow felt the same trying to contain his anxiety while waiting for his departure. On the third day, he helped fill sandbags to reline the outside of his hut because it took his mind off the nighttime and added a few more pounds of protection. The work and nightly mortar attacks drained his strength and ambition until he collapsed on his rack in the late afternoon and fell into a deep sleep. In the early morning hours, he dreamt he was awake with the siren wailing and the thuds of incoming mortars cratering in his brain. However, as dreams go, he could not move, could not get out of the way or wake up until the siren faded and the bursts of blasting shells no longer punctuated his chaotic, semi-conscious sleep.

After the all clear, someone turned on the lights and the other men looked incredulously at Cow still lying in his bunk unstirred. He awoke then and looked back at those around him who marveled at his composure in the face of death. For his part, he was not sure which was worse, the dream or the reality, and got up to go out and relieve himself.

At breakfast, the talk was all about the three nights of mortars and casualties in the area. With the amount of ammunition moved, day and night, it was a wonder to most that a bigger blast had not occurred. A couple guys joked about it, but that was because they were leaving in a few

195

minutes. Cow, down to one and a wakeup, was determined to keep his ass low for the next 48 hours.

Filling more sandbags consumed the fourth morning and Cow spent the afternoon at the flight center verifying his departure date and securing a seat. Later, the first round on his penultimate night was even closer than usual with the shrapnel pinging on the metal roof as it dropped. By the last ping, Cow was again under his bunk, slid all the way back against the sandbagged wall. This time there were only two shells, two explosions, two reminders that they were still out there at two in the morning. "The bastards..." Cow said to himself as he waited under his bed for the clearing siren. Across the floor and through the screen door, he could see the night, bright with dropping flares. A helicopter churned nearby, and, for a moment, he picked up the drone of a DC-3 before Puff's distinctive buzz began. Nonetheless, there was no need to crawl out to help or hinder the cause. Just keep down and stay low, he reminded himself, no need to step in it now.

Puff slipped out of Cow's conscience as the parachuted flares burned down. He listened carefully, but the chopper had faded away too and still, no one seemed to make an effort to crawl out from under his rack. Finally, however, "Jeeze-us Key-riest," came from beneath one bunk bed. "I'm caught on the springs and can't get out of here!"

"That's what you get for trying to hump your pillow," said a second voice.

"Is that the voice of experience?" asked the first. "I think my flak jacket is caught. Can't get loose without tipping over the whole damn thing. Give me a hand!"

Someone near the door turned on the lights and Cow could see by his Timex that it was nearly half past two. He was still looking at his watch when the first bunk bed went over causing a domino effect. In the next isle, five bunks toppled with three or four yelling soldiers buried beneath.

"Now get ME out of here," yelled the second voice.

"How ya like it now?" laughed the first. "And any guy who grabs for a pillow gets extended!"

The second voice pushed the bed off and jumped up, grabbing the closest pillow he could find. In a wide arc, he swung at the head and mouth of the first voice, but before contact the pillowcase snagged on an upturned metal leg and the ticking tore open with an explosion of feathers.

"You dumb ass," screamed the first voice before starting to laugh. Cow could see the white shrapnel float down onto the floor as three more soldiers pushed their way out of the toppled mess and grabbed for pillows too. The second voice was nearly choking in laughter as the soft thuds of pillows smacked him repeatedly causing more feathers to fly helter-skelter.

The second voice kept repeating, half-shouting, half-laughing, "Hump this, hump that!" as pillows burst around him and feathers flew everywhere.

The floor was nearly white when the screen door squealed in opening and a voice yelled, "Attent-HUT!" Immediately, the scuffling, wheezing laughter and muffled mayhem came to a stop as the officer came forward. "What in God's name is going on in here?" he asked. "Just because you think you're going home doesn't mean you have a right to destroy government property. I'm going to write down your names, ranks and serial numbers and you're going to clean up this mess if it takes another enlistment to do it. DO I MAKE MYSELF CLEAR?"

"YES, SIR!" was the united response except for Cow who was still under his bunk listening to the scratch of the pencil on paper as each of the soldiers, standing at attention, gave name, rank, and serial number.

"I'll be back in forty-five minutes to check on your progress and I expect this place to be shipshape!" The door hinges squealed again as the officer of the day departed and the closing spring twanged in rebuttal. A moment later someone said, "Damn, that certainly was extraordinary!" and muffled laughter began again as the bunks were tipped upright and the feathers swept into poncho liners.

In fifteen minutes, the only remaining feather was caught on Cow's helmet liner where he lay sleeping under his bunk. He never knew if the OD came back, but, when he awoke in the morning, sunlight was coming through the screen door and his neck and back ached from sleeping on the floor wearing a helmet and lumpy flak jacket. Sliding out from under the bed, he shed the gear and stretched out on his mattress like the others in the hut—four down and one to go.

XXXII

Welcome Home

The C-130 came in low over East Da Nang bringing winter with it. The airplane, flying northwest toward a small island in the middle of the river, apparently released its load too soon dropping the snow behind it. Low, the sudden roar of its engines was as startling as the white swirls in its prop wash. Churned overhead, the cool saturated air came down in a whiteout that settled on everything and mixed with the mud.

The airplane was already well beyond the island when Cow stepped back, under the shop roof, to watch the rest of the flakes float to earth. It was all over in a minute or two as the fallen snow dissipated, dissolved and evaporated, until any evidence that it had ever fallen was as removed as the aircraft that dropped it. It was an odd occurrence, even for Vietnam, where oddity was the regimen.

No one knew for sure what the white flakes were but the consensus was Agent Orange aimed at the island vegetation. Why it came down in flakes instead of mist or vapor was anyone's guess. One notion was that the heat of the day caused a chemical reaction with the kerosene or diesel fuel used to dilute it. Another was that the prop wash cooled it until the droplets turned to flakes. But it really made no difference because there was nothing to be done about it anyway. It happened, was over and spread everywhere.

Watching it come down, Cow envisioned an invading orange army hanging under miniscule white parachutes. After the hit and roll, the chutes collapsed and the paratroopers disappeared into the quagmire. Cow was going to disappear too because it was lunchtime and he was only waiting for the sky to clear. When it finally did, he brushed off his hair and shoulders, pulled on his soft cap and stepped into the morass of mud on his way to chow.

The Boss sat on a bar stool smoking a cigarette and nursing a beer. Behind the bar, Buddy washed glasses and put them upside down on the drain board to dry. Buddy did not talk much in the morning but was still quick to take care of customers who needed an eye opener or had a little time to waste. He would listen to the bar talk when needed, but, if he had heard enough, often walked out and let his wife take over.

The actual bar was a deep brown color, almost black and worn smooth by years of use. The back bar was the same matching color with a smoke glazed mirror in the middle that filtered everything coming in or going out. In a hazy reflection, The Boss watched Cow enter wearing his black Navy pea coat. Double breasted, the coat had a big collar and large plastic buttons with anchors stamped into them. Resurrected for the Wisconsin winter, it was the only thing from his seabag that Cow still used. His hair, what was left of it, had grown to shoulder length and he covered his head with a plush black Cossack style hat pulled down to his eyebrows.

The hats were popular on college campuses where the Vietnam War was not.

The Boss knew Cow and had offered him a job when he came back from Vietnam. Cow, had turned him down, though, saying he wanted to go to school, to college, and that had soured the relationship for some reason. Now, back on winter break, his long hair and hat adding insult to injury, The Boss did not even acknowledge his presence.

Buddy placed a PBR on the bar in front of Cow and went back to his glasses. Nearly everyone drank Pabst Blue Ribbon in Hillton and Cow was no exception. "When in Rome...." He was not a kid anymore and of legal drinking age, 21, with two tours in Vietnam behind him, two quarters in college completed, and way to much of a receding hairline. The G.I. bill was paying for school but to make ends meet, he tended bar part-time at a college hangout. He knew the ropes although they were sometimes more tangled and knotted in his hometown.

Buddy kept washing glasses with half his attention on a television in a far back corner. It was a black and white set with no sound that he usually watched when the place was empty. Some said that he could read lips and did not need the sound. Others insisted that he could not read at all and, except for the drop of a quarter on the bar, could not hear anything either. Whichever, he was staying low for the moment because The Boss did not like Cow and Cow's attitude matched his antisocial hat and long, thin hair. Bent over,

Buddy kept his hands to his task with one eye aimed at the silent TV in the distance. He had heard it all before and was going to keep out of it even if he had to wash the same glasses several times over.

In a few minutes, however, the chance meeting ended and the tension quickly dissolved. Cow had only been killing time waiting for a haircut in the barbershop across the street, and, downing the beer, he left the empty bottle and an extra quarter on the bar when he stepped out. Jaywalking, he entered the barbershop at the appointed time and sat down in the chair with a joking comment about paying half price for half a cut. He added, "I used to think it was hereditary but both my grandfathers had full heads of hair all their lives—my dad too, still does. Guess it's from Nam. They dumped some shit on us in Da Nang and every time I combed my hair after that, it came out by the comb full. Still does but there ain't much left, is there? Well, the cap keeps my head warm even if it pisses off some people around here."

The barber only nodded. "Cut or trim," he asked, more to his mirror and counter than his customer.

"Just trim it up," said Cow, as a cape settled over his shoulders and was buttoned at the back of his neck.

The barber used his comb in one hand—a little harshly, Cow thought, as it scraped his scalp—and a scissors in the other. He had heard Cow but did not care to listen. Vietnam was a conflict, everyone knew that, and the whole thing was getting old—not even a real war. Besides, he hated cutting long hair and his local Legion would not even let these guys in. Sometimes he wondered why he did. What would a longhaired hippie know about war? Guadalcanal had been war and trims were $5.50, same as a cut. After a long pause in his thinking, he finally said, "Looks like a little snow is coming."

XXXIII

Pails in Comparison

Nearly every soldier who traveled up or down Highway 1, south of Da Nang, saw the pails. Some of the soldiers winced, others cracked jokes, but hardly anybody missed seeing them. The open buckets were carried on shoulder poles, one step at a time, in a slow elongated procession that, like the war, never seemed to have a real beginning or conclusion.

Small, thin women were generally the beasts of burden along the highway. The women, or girls, were so skinny that most of the time it was unclear if they were actually female, but that is how they were dressed. They wore black satin pants down to their tire-soled sandals unless they walked barefooted in the sand and gravel. Long sleeved blouses, usually in pink, lavender or white, made up the rest of their uniform along with the almost mandatory straw hat. Walking, one arm swung with the stride of their steps while the other balanced the pole that flexed up and down in rhythm with their movement. From a distance, the conical straw hats appeared to be caps on balancing scales where shoulders formed the fulcrums and pails of equal weight dangled from the tips of the poles. Except for the forward momentum, they might have been made of brass.

Most soldiers did not look into the pails for long because it made their stomachs turn. Pink strands swirled on top with yellow chunks floating freely like a vomit stew. It was more pink than yellow, but so nauseating in appearance that no one wanted to get any closer. The pails of goop simply dared and defied inspection as the procession went on unexamined. For the most part, it was unexamined and unfettered until forty years later, when, in a moment of recollection and clarity, without ever having looked, Cow knew exactly what was in those buckets beneath the slop on top. The contraband had gone right by beneath turned noses and only needed to be dumped in the ditch where the mines, grenades, ammunition and communication pouches would have spread across the sand like the guts of our guys from the Mekong Delta to the DMZ.

Near the fortieth anniversary of the Tet Offensive, a retired American General appeared on NBC's *Today Show* after having pedaled his bicycle the length of Vietnam down Highway 1. He was on television to promote his book detailing the journey from Hanoi in the north to Ho Chi Minh City (Saigon) in the south and spoke of meeting some of the people he had opposed during the war. In essence, he talked of his personal growth, well removed from that troubled time. Unfortunately, what he said was about as damning as anything ever voiced about the Vietnam War. Basically, 40 years later, what he learned on his ride south was that the Vietnamese people of the time did not care whether they were democratic, socialistic or communistic, as long as the killing of their children and the bombing and burning of their homes and crops would stop. What is unfathomable is that it took this military leader four decades to learn what many observers and participants could readily have told him in 1968. Perhaps, at the time, because of his elevated leadership position, he was too far removed from the pails on the shoulder poles. But equally perplexing is that being in the proximity of the pails, essentially right on top of them, did not help much either. We stumbled in, stumbled out, and only in hindsight recognize some of the tripwires, bare threads and loose ends.

Cover design is a rendition of the ribbon for the

Vietnam Service Medal